DISCORDANT

Mia Dalia

Advance Praise:

"A young man in a dead-end job who dreams of rock stardom discovers a literally magical path to realize his desire…but at what cost? Mia Dalia's *Discordant* is an unsettling and fascinating tale of the supernatural."

—Arthur Shattuck O'Keefe, author of *The Spirit Phone*

"*Discordant* is a captivating tale about life, death, good, evil, and the power of rock and roll. I was completely hooked from the start, and not just because one of the main characters is a Martin D-28 dreadnought acoustic guitar. *Discordant* is ostensibly the story of Jax, a former bartender and club musician who is forced to leave the life he loves, take a menial job, and move back into his mother's basement after he gets a girl pregnant. Now he is a young man who hates his life and resents the baby and fate for putting him in that position. He works at a local retirement community, where he meets Mr. Chambers, one of the long-term residents. As time goes by, he discovers Mr. Chambers happens to own a classic Martin D-28, the same type of guitar as Jax's music hero, Aaron Chase of the band Dreadnought, used to play. As tiny clues start to mount, Jax finds himself pondering the impossible – could this octogenarian patient who can hardly speak somehow be the decades younger Chase, who disappeared mysteriously after releasing his greatest song? In the end, Jax not only discovers the truth but also confronts his own mortality and faces a choice that could change his entire world.

Mia Dalia's writing is enthralling; her use of language keeps you turning page after page, not only to see what happens but to enjoy its effortless beauty. She creates characters you want to know. and her plot is like a rafting down a river: it starts gently enough but without warning turns into a ride that moves faster and faster until you shoot over the falls. The proof of this book's magic is that I was reading it at night and had to stay up until well after midnight to finish it because I couldn't wait until the next day. *Discordant* is a fresh new take on a story as old as country blues."

– JG Faherty, author of *Songs in the Key of Death, Ragman,* and *The Wakening*

The thing about Mia Dalia is her ability to understand people. The way she can turn an anti-hero into someone you are on the edge-of-your-seat rooting for. Here we see how protagonist Jax loses his way in life. A guy with a schoolboy dream, he's desperate to keep alive, but who hates the world because of the repercussions from his wayward tomfoolery. The monster of regret continually hangs over him. Until he meets Mr Chambers …

What could be a downward spiral tale of a man wanting revenge on the world turns into something that is anything but. It's an emotionally driven story that is touching in parts, and feeds hope to us all that those dreams we assumed to be unattainable, well, with a little bit of magic, perhaps they're not as forgotten as we all once thought.

Mia Dalia has a style I've fallen in love with. She's the lovechild of Caroline Kepnes and Gillian Flynn, with her unapologetic narrative and gritty honesty. Her words flow like an emo song that captures each feeling as if it is our own.

Discordant is a little bit of *Crossroads*, and dash of *Trick or Treat*, but mostly it's pure brilliance. A fantastic read and without a shadow of doubt is now one of my favourite authors!

-Jim Ody, author of *The Place That Never Existed, Little Miss Evil,* and *Lost Connections*.

CONTENTS

For

Chelsea

DISCORDANT

The smallest things can change your life. The smallest, tiniest, stupidest mistakes. This used to be an abstract notion to Jax once–nothing but a movie cliché—until life went and made an example out of him. And now here he was, with nothing but time to contemplate it, as he emptied bedpans and scrubbed cheap linoleum floors. Things turn on a dime, his grandpa used to say. For Jax, that dime turned out to be a broken condom.

Of all the Seth Rogen movies he'd watched—and there were many, he was very much a fan—if asked which one he'd prefer to find himself in, he'd certainly never choose *Knocked Up*. Maybe *Long Shot* or something, definitely not *Knocked*

Up. Yet, here he was, living in an inferior, unflavored by cheap sentimentality and rom-com tropes, version of *Knocked Up.* And hating every minute of it.

He didn't even know Maggie all that well. She was a girl—no, a young woman—who came to the bar he used to work at from time to time. She sang along to his band's songs when they played, pouring their hearts out on the sticky makeshift stages at the same bar or ones just like it around town. She was someone he'd seen around and occasionally went home with. They never talked about anything meaningful. They merely kept each other company some nights. That's all. They had no understanding about their relationship—as far as Jax was concerned there was no relationship to have an understanding about. He saw other people, of course he did. What else was the point of being young and in a band and having a job slinging drinks at a popular dive bar? He presumed Maggie did too. To be honest, he didn't think much about her when she wasn't right in front of him. Sure, she was cute, with the sort of fresh sunny good looks that were never going to survive the test of time, but so were many girls. Jax didn't even know her last name until it was much too late.

The day Maggie told him she was pregnant, his feelings oscillated between righteous indignation (was this kid even his?) and frustrated resignation (sure, I'll help pay for the abortion). He couldn't fathom option number three. Certainly, didn't think Maggie would either. And yet...funny how these things go.

Must be genetic, must be social conditioning, must be hormonal—*something*; something told Maggie that having this kid was a good idea and that was that. And now Jax was on an eighteen-year hook of having to pay for someone's condom manufacturing mistake and someone's urge to reproduce.

He tried reasoning with Maggie—Wouldn't she prefer waiting to have a kid until she's in a proper relationship, etc.?—but she looked at him like they were suddenly speaking different languages. Said she didn't expect him to be around unless he wanted to. But she did expect money.

No more bar work, Jax had to go get whatever passed for a *real job*, which for a college dropout aspiring musician with bartending experience, meant menial labor. His mom pulled some strings, and here he was—a janitor in an old people's home. No more band either, he could no longer get the free practice/performance space through work, and, frankly, he was just too tired these days for rock'n'roll life. Jax tried balancing the two but quickly became aware that he was playing like shit, and, worst of all, his bandmates knew it too. So that was that. He went from being someone he loved being and living the life he loved living to this: an aspiration-free janitor staying, like a cheap cliché, in his mom's basement to save money. Money, the lion's share of which he had to hand over each month for the upkeep of the baby he had nothing to do with. *Wanted* nothing to do with.

Jax paused and used the mop bucket's wringer to squeeze out the dirty water. It was the same grey as the linoleum; the same grey as the skies outside—the perpetual threat of rain that translated into increased humidity. The place was depressing no matter how you looked at it. Even smelled depressing. Its proper name was the Cherry Orchard Active Retirement Community. There was indeed a small cherry orchard on the premises, though which came first, the name or the trees, Jax didn't know.

What he did know was that they charged exorbitant rates to take care of the old-timers who either had no families or whose families wanted nothing to do with them. And sure, there were plenty of activities on hand to justify the 'Active' part of the official assignation, but it didn't exactly distract from the knowledge that people came here to die. It seemed oddly appropriate—or maybe ironic, Jax was never sure on the proper use of irony—that this was the place his dreams came to die too.

A piercing voice shredded his reverie. "Jackson? Jackson, you here?"

Walk around the corner and see for yourself, thought Jax. He cringed involuntarily, like he did every time he heard that heavy Brooklyn accent, but immediately made the effort of covering it up with a smile. It wouldn't do to piss off the boss.

Donna Collodi was the string his mother pulled to get him the job. The two knew each other somehow, either through their stich'n'bitch knitting circle or a book club or something. They weren't close, but then again, you wouldn't give a job like this to the son of your best friend. For the son of a casual acquaintance, it was a perfectly reasonable favor.

Jax didn't know if he hated Donna per se—hate was a strong emotion, and he generally wasn't huge on those. Strong dislike was probably more appropriate. There was something infuriating about her pinched wrinkled face, her grating voice, sure, but it was the talking that got to him the most. The woman simply never shut up. She also, to Jax's best recollection, never said a single interesting thing. The combination was a doozy.

Donna Collodi had run The Cherry Orchard for the past two decades. Her own mother was living here, presumably at a discount. As far as Jax knew, that was her only family.

When he first met Donna, she seemed friendly enough, but there was always an underlying current of toxicity present. Staying away wasn't an option either—she was his boss. A boss prone to giving him extraneous tasks as if to challenge his commitment to the job. And still, even emptying bedpans was preferable to being stuck in a conversation with the woman. Both tasks were inherently unpleasant, but the former was at least time-limited, the latter could go on indefinitely. Always some small grievances with the '*clients*' as they were supposed to call them, or their families, or other employees. And gossip, gossip, mountains of gossip.

When Jax first got the job, drinking with his best friend after hours was the only way he could cope. Deek stayed the course of the idle life: continuing to work at the same bar, crashing in the house with four other guys, still playing in the band. Deek was fortunate. His condoms didn't break, he didn't become a cautionary tale of a misspent youth. To Deek, Jax's new life was wildly exotic, though not in a way he'd ever want to partake in. More like a spectator sport.

"Just think how dumb of a name that is," Jax said, sipping his beer, regretfully waving away the offer of a joint since the Cherry Orchard's employees were subject to random tests. "I mean, her family's Italian; she's Italian. In Italian, Donna means Lady or, like, Mrs. or Madam. That's like someone in Berlin naming their kid Frau."

"Or like someone in Madrid naming their kid Señora."

"So, if she were ever in Italy, she'd be Donna Donna Collodi."

"Imagine a new character on *Downton Abbey* named Lady Lady."

They both laughed.

"Wait, dude, you watch *Downton*? Is that what you're telling me?"

"Nah, it's just always on at the Cherry. The olds love that shit. It's like their *Game of Thrones*."

"Riiight …."

"Oh, shut up, you moppet. It's good to have a wide span of popular cultural references."

More laughter ensued.

"That is some serious failure of imagination on her parent's behalf, though, isn't it? Like looking at their newborn and going … whaddaya wanna call it? I dunno. I mean, it's a female child, and we're Italian, so why not just. .." Deek chortled, taking a toke.

"Yeah, well, she rides my ass. She's like the freaking dictator of that place, all five feet nothing of her."

"Napoleonic complex".

"Something like that. That place is like her entire life. I bet she has her own room somewhere on the premises, so she doesn't even have to leave."

"Remember that old song about a Donna?"

Jax searched his memory. "Ritchie Valens?"

"That's the one." Deek started singing. He'd always had a good voice, surprisingly melodic, almost crooner-like, though the songs their band played seldom required that quality.

"Wonder if his Donna was Italian too," Jax said, crushing his beer can.

Now Donna Donna Collodi was before him; her dyed blonde hair a nimbus around her small, wrinkled face. He couldn't tell exactly how old she was, between the chemical blondness, the raisin-like skin, and the caffeine-fueled energy.

"Jackson, I'm glad I found you. Could you do me a favor and look in on Mr. Chambers? Missy is late for her shift, and we are just a bit shorthanded at the moment."

Translation: Missy still can't get her shit together and show up for work on time, and Mr. Chambers needs his bedpan emptied. And though this isn't Jax's job, he'll have to do it anyway.

He once read his official job description, and it mentioned nothing directly about interacting with or taking care of the clients, but it did feature something that read "additional duties performed as requested" in very small print. That's how they got you, the powers that be—small print.

And then they owned you.

"Of course." Jax nodded with artificial amicability. Of all the old farts in here, Mr. Chambers was one of the nicer ones. Quietly looney, he might leave feces, but he'd never fling them. Small mercies.

"Thank you, Jackson." His boss wouldn't call him Jax resolutely, even after he asked her to. He had stopped asking since. "I don't know what I'd do without you. You know, Missy is on her last warning. I'm sympathetic to her situation with the kids, but this is too much. This new guy she's been seeing …"

And there went a good ten to fifteen minutes of Jax's life. There was no stopping Donna once she got going; you just had to wait it out or hope a distraction might present itself. Eventually, she was paged to the reception area, and Jax was released.

He made his way to the second floor. Mr. Chambers' room was the last one on the left. On a smaller side, but with a nice view of the orchard. A slice of the sky, too. Not much really, but as far as Jax could tell, the man wasn't all there, not enough to need more.

"Hi, Mr. Chambers, remember me? I'm Jax. I heard you needed some assistance?"

Jax never liked interacting with the clients. They reminded him of his own mortality in a way that made him uncomfortable. By the flip side of that coin, the baby—*his son*, he had to remind himself—should have made him feel immortal, but never did. From the first time Jax laid eyes on the tiny red wrinkled visage of the swaddled bundle to this day, the baby felt … alien to him. He saw nothing of himself in him, felt nothing of himself in it. Jax wondered what it said about him—was he a sociopath? Did he not yawn when others did? Why couldn't he melt in the presence of the baby the way Maggie did, the way his mom did? Why did this mean nothing to him?

When he was younger, he used to think that he'd achieve immortality through his music, and then, as years brought some reality-flavored clarity, he stopped thinking that, stopped thinking about immortality at all. Not everyone was meant to leave a legacy, he figured. Nothing wrong with just living in the now, enjoying what's around for as long as it's around. The baby—*his son*—was now his legacy. If not an embodiment of all his hopes and dreams, then at least a continuation of his genetic material. Jax wished it mattered more.

Maybe in time, he thought, once the baby grows and becomes more of a person, someone with ideas and opinions … maybe. But he wouldn't bet on it.

Whatever he felt when he was with the baby, something like bewildered curiosity, didn't go too far in mitigating the burning resentment he otherwise felt toward the entire situation. The rest was difficult to put into words.

Consequently, Jax didn't spend too much time with his son, didn't even get to have a say in naming him; certainly wouldn't have voted for Jeffrey given half a chance. What sort of a stupid bland name was that? A family name, he was told, Maggie's grandpa. Well, okay then.

Mr. Chambers looked about a thousand years old. Ancient, wizened. The kind of old where you can't tell—can't even believe—this person was ever young. Parchment-thin skin, near translucent, wisps of gossamer-like white hairs around an otherwise bald, age-marked pate, stooped bony shoulders, shaking hands folded in his lap, the old man sat in a plaid-upholstered, comfortable-looking wingchair by the window. He seemed lost in thought, slowly nodding to himself, and didn't pause to acknowledge Jax's arrival.

The room was a standard mid-range suite. Mr. Chambers or his family must have had *some* money. It was anonymously accommodating in a way of a nicer hotel with surprisingly few personal touches. Most people here brought too much with them, having to downsize an entire lifetime into a suitcase or two. Mr. Chambers, it seemed, was a minimalist. There were some books; Jax browsed the spines, nothing he'd read, only obscure history tomes. Some DVDs much in the same vein. A framed photo of a family without Mr. Chambers in it. And, in the corner, incongruously, a guitar. Jax got close to examine it—it was a Martin. A beautiful older acoustic Martin D-28, it had to have been worth a pretty penny. Johnny Cash played one like that, Elvis too, McCartney; so many of the greats.

Jax had never played a Martin, never even held one, and now that he was so close to it, the pull was irresistible. He picked up the guitar, reverently, and strummed a few chords. Surprisingly, it was in tune. He couldn't imagine Mr. Chambers' shaky age-gnarled hands tuning an instrument, let alone playing it. The Martin sounded beautiful, resonant, devastatingly melodic. What Jax wouldn't do for a guitar like that. Why couldn't that be the small thing his life pivoted on, not a stupid broken condom? What kind of a musician might he have become with a guitar like that? He'd never know now.

In fact, just playing the Martin, he knew he was breaking the rules; Donna would have a conniption if she saw him.

One more minute and he'll put it back, he told himself. And that's when he heard Mr. Chambers humming, ever so softly. It sounded strangely, hauntingly familiar, and yet frustratingly unplaceable. The old man turned his head so that he was facing Jax, and there was something in his watery pale blue eyes, something like great sadness tinged with an even greater fear. He extended his shaking finger at Jax and said, quietly, but distinctly, "No, no, don't."

Jax put the guitar back immediately, apologized. The last thing he wanted was a client complaint on his record.

He set about emptying the bedpan and straightening out the room. It didn't take long. He apologized again, and just as he was getting ready to head out, noticed Mr. Chambers' shoulders shaking. Jax looked closer and saw tears making their way down the age-etched ravines of the old man's face and soundlessly landing into his blanket-clad lap.

"Are you okay, Mr. Chambers?" Jax asked, but there was no answer. He'd gone and upset the old man, though he never meant to. Jax left his room, annoyed at himself, annoyed at having been there in the first place. This is exactly why he didn't interact with the clients. He'd never upset a toilet or a window, even when he used the wrong kind of cleaner. He didn't want to be responsible for anyone's tears. Didn't like responsibility in general and avoided it whenever possible.

Jax walked away, shaking his head. Despite his irritation, he could still feel the Martin in his hands, the sheer somatic joy of playing an instrument like that. He found himself humming and realized it was the very melody Mr. Chambers hummed. How strange, he thought, it was only a few chords worth of music, a snippet, really, but it stayed with him throughout the day all the same.

When Jax got home—at a reasonable hour for a change—his mom was in the living room. So was the baby. His mom was going for the grandmother-of-the-year once again, doting on Jeffrey, cooing to him. Jax sighed and prepared for the inevitable and sure enough …

"Wash up and take the baby, hon, he's been waiting for his daddy for hours."

Why the voice? Why does everyone speak in that voice around babies? So, they can grow up with a totally bizarre and wrong concept of what adults sound like?

Jax washed his hands in the kitchen sink, splashed some water on his face. Couldn't find the kitchen towel, so he used a couple of napkins from the cow-shaped napkin holder on the kitchen table. Then went and dutifully took Jeffrey from his mom, cradling his arms just as she taught him to support the baby's head.

The kid looked at him with something like distant bemusement, like he couldn't quite place him, and then, apparently, did, because he screwed up his pink face and let out a piercing wail—his standard reaction to Jax.

"He doesn't see you enough," his mother clucked. "He forgets what you look like."

"Maybe he remembers and just doesn't like me."

"Don't say that. Of course, he likes you. You're his dad."

More like an unwitting sperm donor/lifelong sponsor, Jax wanted to say but didn't. He handed the baby back to his mom. "I'm tired. Had a long day. You mind?"

"Mind? Of course, I don't mind. Why would I mind spending time with my favorite lil' guy?" More of that baby goochygoo voice.

"You hungry, hon? I can make you a sandwich."

"Nah, thanks. I had something earlier, I'm good". Jax headed toward his basement room, the cliché of all clichés, albeit comfortable enough.

The baby was calming down, but slowly. Jax closed the door. As he descended the stairs, Jeffrey's cries mercifully receded.

His place was what a realtor would euphemistically call a 'daylight basement' due to a couple of windows that just barely cleared the ground level and occasionally—reluctantly—did let in some light if the sun angled itself just right. But the sun was long gone for the day, so Jax turned on the overhead light which came on with a buzz. The basement had its own en-suite bathroom and a makeshift kitchenette. The furniture was a series of discards from upstairs: an old table, an older futon, a beat-up recliner permanently stuck in the reclined position. The only newish things were a flatscreen TV, a gaming console, and a laptop, and even those were pretty dated by the impossible-to-keep-up-with rapid pace of technological evolution.

Jax poured himself a bowl of store-brand Fruity Loops. Milk, beer, and condiments were just about the only things in his mini fridge, which also served as a microwave stand. He turned on his TV and booted up his gaming system; the massive noise-canceling headphones went on next, obscuring all ambient sound. Eating cereal while wearing those beastly things sounded insane, like working in a rock quarry would, he imagined. But alas, it beat the alternatives. This way he was firmly and completely ensconced in his own world.

Amid the artificial fruit flavor and artificial war machine noises, Jax blissfully zoned out.

"You should really spend more time with him," his mom told him next morning as he was heading out to work. "He's going to think you don't love him."

He'd be right to. "He's not going to think anything, ma. He doesn't *think*, he's a baby. He just eats and poops and sleeps."

Oddly enough, every so often, Jax did catch Jeffrey looking at him funny, wrinkling his tiny face into something resembling intelligence or, at least, consideration. In those times, the kid looked just like Benjamin Button the Final Edition—an old man wise with experience, bewildered at the inappropriately tiny and useless form he found himself in and the giants all around him. But then Jax would blink, the image would dissolve, and there would be that blank stare and the wailing again and nothing more.

"I know you didn't plan on having him, Jax, hon." *Oh, here we go again.* "But now that he's here, don't you care about him? Isn't he adorable?"

Jax wished he could love as easily as others did, as easily as his mom did. His mom was a veritable fount of love, a genuinely warm and bubbly person, whose heart was melted easily and readily by babies, puppies, cheesy movies, all that nonsense.

Jax was … well, different. Sure, he loved his mom. Loved his dad too, he supposed, or at least the memory of the man too long gone now for details to remain. He was fond of his friends, especially Deek. But he had never been in love and was beginning to think it might not be in the cards for him. Surely, it wasn't some sort of a mandatory thing for everyone. Surely, it couldn't have been as simple as not having met the right girl yet, as his mother believed.

He often thought about what his life could have been like had he loved Maggie, had he loved Jeffrey. But he didn't know if it would have been a *better* life. Maybe just a very different one.

It was much more fun to entertain the possibility of, say, music stardom. If the band had hit it big, if their songs were on the radio, if they toured. Now *that* was definitively a better life than the one he was currently stuck in. And Jax walked away from it, walked away from even the slightest chance of it, to push a mop for a paycheck around people waiting for death. Boy, did it piss him off.

The Cherry Orchard was brimming with activity that day. Something about a concert some local kids were putting on for the old-timers. There were chairs to rearrange, tables to move, a stage to set up. Jax tried to ignore the irony. Then tried to amuse himself by imagining the senior citizens rocking out to his band's tunes. His *former* band's tunes, he corrected himself.

They were probably never going to be famous, if he was to be honest with himself. They never had that elusive IT factor. They had angst that matured into righteous anger that translated quite well into the rock-tinged metal or metal-tinged rock they played, but that was about it. Still, it was fun; it was *so much* fun. To be up there, on a stage, any stage, to watch people be moved by something you did, see them rocking out to your music, syncing to your beat…it was the best feeling in the world. If he continued being honest with himself, it might have been better than sex. Not something he'd ever admit out loud, but there it was.

Festive didn't look right amid the Cherry Orchard's walls, but the effort was made. The kids were, admittedly, cute; middle-schoolers singing their young hearts out, voices prepubescently high and crystal clear. The old folks seemed to enjoy it. Jax was helping out with turning the impromptu concert arena back into the dining room when Donna appeared out of nowhere asking him to help. Once again, outside of his job description's remit. And once again, he said nothing, because, frankly, escorting Mr. Chambers back to his suite was infinitely preferable to enduring another Donna-style rant/monologue. She did squeeze in some morsels, something about the new elevator repairman being rude to her or…Jax tuned her out. Mr. Chambers appeared to be exhausted by his afternoon's outing, so Jax hustled getting him back before he was liable to pass out.

The old man could barely walk by himself. Jax wondered why he hadn't opted for a wheelchair that day. Many clients in the home did, even if they still had some mobility left in them. Right now, he was walking—well, barely ambulating—by himself, but leaning most of his weight on Jax for support. Mr. Chambers was heavier then he looked. It must have been his height, imposing even after the shrinking that comes with age. Jax struggled to maintain his balance, but in the end, he managed to get the old man back to his room successfully.

The poor guy was beat, with barely enough energy to gesture to his chair, so that's where Jax planted him. Mr. Chambers' mouth was doing that trembly thing that sometimes was a prelude for speaking and sometimes just a twitch. Either way, Jax leaned in.

"Water." Such a weak thin voice. Barely audible, like a distant wind through the reeds.

Jax fetched the old man some water and helped him with the glass. He got a slight nod of thanks in return.

The room was stifling with heat and stale, recycled air.

"Would you like your sweater off, Mr. Chambers?" Jax asked. During his time at the Cherry Orchard, he learned to presume nothing. The elderly seemed to never be warm enough. Thin blood or something.

The old man nodded again. Jax leaned him forward ever so slightly and removed the cardigan, one sleeve at a time. Beneath it was a crisp white short-sleeve shirt. It looked ironed and starched. Jax couldn't remember the last time he wore an ironed shirt. His work uniform was made from cheap wrinkle-free material. His outside-of-work attire consisted almost entirely of band T-shirts and jeans.

That wasn't what attracted his attention though—it was the ink. Mr. Chambers' arms were heavily tattooed up and down, sleeved in art. All ruinous with age now, like a PSA announcement about the consequences of youthful follies, but once upon a time, it must have looked something fierce.

"Nice ink, Mr. Chambers," Jax nodded approvingly, unable to look away from the faded designs weaving in and out through the crepe-thin wrinkled skin and sparse, coarse white arm hair. He could make out some images more clearly than others. One, in particular, looked so very familiar. Or maybe he was merely imagining things, seeing patterns when none were to be found. Wasn't there a word for that? Either way, the old man looked beat. So Jax left him to nap by the window and walked away, throwing a longing look to the Martin in the corner.

Jax shouldn't have come. He knew it as soon as he set foot in the place; a notion that continued to reinforce itself throughout the evening, alcohol consumed notwithstanding.

He was proving true that old chestnut of not stepping into the same river twice. Funny thing is, he didn't think *he'd* changed all that much. It was all the life around him that did.

This was no longer his bar. This was no longer his place. There was a new bartender behind the weathered oak counter—that much was expected. Some joker with spiderwebs tattoos on his elbows and a dyed fauxhawk. Okay, fine.

But then the band, his former band, started setting up, and Jax noticed that he'd already been replaced there too. The new guy was tall, lean, wiry-muscled with a flinty-eyed-don't-give-a-toss rock'n'roll look Jax had tried perfecting in a mirror so many times. He wore a sleeveless black T-shirt with 'Sex Sells' on it in red lettering and a pair of ripped black jeans.

Jax caught Deek's eye, and Deek, at least, had the decency to throw him a helpless 'sorry, but what can I do' shrug. Still, it was strange, surreal even, to find oneself so easily replaceable. It certainly didn't bode well for one's self-esteem.

Jax downed his shot and asked for another. Someone—a server?—must have clued Fauxhawk in on who Jax was, and Fauxhawk tried to make small talk. Jax made the effort to maintain his scowl on the right side of the can-pass-for-a-smile expression and accepted a free drink. He couldn't quite stop looking at the new bandmate setting up. The guy obviously knew what he was doing. The stringy muscles of his arms rippled as he moved, as he tuned his guitar, quickly running through some scales. His hair was long and carelessly tossed like it didn't matter, but Jax was sure it was strategic and made for a killer headbanging motion.

Once they started playing, Jax skulked back to the farthest corner of the bar. They were good, the sound was good, the new guy was good—he had to admit that. And it stung. The cheap booze did nothing to soothe it. Not really.

Jax tried to imagine it was him up there, in the shoddy spotlight on that ersatz stage. His fingers automatically began running through the chord progression of the song the band was currently playing, one of their biggest hits, according to their audience, anyway. And then he realized that he was simply too tired for it, too tired to be the guy up there, strolling and strumming and sweating way past midnight, until they were out of songs and the crowd out of energy and the bar out of time.

Jax, the working man, had *maybe* another beer in him

before dragging his sorry ass back home and passing out in front of the TV. The sad reality of it all dawned like a rude awakening. He shook his head with anger, looked around, and spotted Tori a few feet over. She smiled and raised her beer bottle at him, before taking a sip.

Tori was a regular. Jax knew her professionally—and, on occasion, carnally—though never well. She was a local tattoo artist with a devout following, older though indeterminably so due to a generally kickass aura she projected. Today her hair was dyed fire-engine red with orange highlights; the result looked like a flame. Unlike every tattoo artist he's ever met, Tori was very selective about the ink she put on her own body and therefore was still in possession of large swaths of unmarked skin territory for future designs. If she chose to dress up, you'd never even know she had any ink at all. Tonight, she was wearing a large men's Ramones T-shirt refashioned as a dress with a metal-studded black leather belt, and a pair of black shit-kicking boots. And jewelry, always lots of custom jewelry, things made of chains and nails—nothing you'd find in a regular jewelry store. Tori's appearance was a statement. Jax liked what it said.

He nodded and lifted his own glass. Took a sip, then slowly made his way over.

"Sitting the show out on the sidelines tonight?" A thin black eyebrow went up, curving like a question mark.

"I…uh…dropped out of the band a while back."

"No shit? I haven't been around in *that* long? Also, why?"

"Long story."

"Abbreviate."

Jax sighed. "I got this stupid job, and there just wasn't enough time anymore, to practice and such."

"Bummer." Tori sipped her beer thoughtfully. "You happier?"

"Not in the slightest."

"Then what gives?"

Jax paused, then decided to tell the truth. "Had a kid."

"No shit?"

"No shit."

They let a beat pass as the song ended.

"Wow. Well, congrats Daddy Jax." Tori smiled and kissed his cheek.

"Yeah, thanks, I guess."

"Not taking to fatherhood?"

"Not really," he admitted. "It's like something in my brain's just missing when it comes to all that. I look at the kid and feel nothing. The kid looks at me and just cries."

He paused for a sip. "Sorry, that's like too much, right? Sorry."

"Don't worry about it. I mean, it's not for everyone. Despite what the popular culture and media want you to believe."

"Ah."

She looked at him appraisingly. "You look different."

"Sadder?"

"Yeah, maybe that's it." Tori smiled. "I always had a thing for sad boys."

"You don't say?" Jax smiled back.

"I do say. You wanna get out of here or stick around and wallow in self-pity some more?"

Jax drained his glass and placed it on the nearest table. "Lead the way."

Tori's apartment was above her tattoo shop and suited her to a tee. The same age-defying wild rock'n'roll awesomeness mixed in with seemingly incongruous proper furnishings—matching, well-made of actual wood—and the occasional original artwork. It wasn't organized per se but had a sort of internal order that made sense to its owner and made it very clear that was the only thing that mattered.

Accordingly, her bed was surprisingly comfortable with clean, sky-blue sheets; an oasis amid the blood-red walls and framed Mike Mignola prints. Jax had been here before, enjoyed it then, and enjoyed it now. He was glad he didn't drink all that much—not enough to affect his performance; glad he mustered up the energy to follow Tori, glad she was into sad boys.

The sex was good, better than even. Something about older women, maybe. Or maybe just something about Tori. In bed, like in life, she moved with the assured confidence of someone who knows exactly what she wants and how to get it. She didn't ask for commitments or meaningless promises; this was purely physical—two adults getting together for the sheer somatic pleasure of it. He made her cum; she told him so and she wouldn't lie about a thing like that. He came too and felt like floating above the sheets, the best he'd felt in a long time—his mind clear, his conscience clearer, his anger at bay.

They lay naked in a puddle of worked-up sweat that was quickly losing its heat, their bodies touching but not quite cuddling as they watched the ceiling fan blades spin.

"What are you going to do about your kid?"

"Nothing much I *can* do. Pay for it until it grows up."

"I was pregnant once," she said whisper-quietly.

Jax turned on his side to face her. "What happened?"

"I was debating getting an abortion, and then nature interfered, and I had a miscarriage."

"Shit. Sorry." Pause. "Would you have gone through with it, you think?"

"I don't know. That's the thing. I think I would have, but I'll never know for sure. We go through life thinking we have all these choices, but the most important choices are often completely out of our control."

It was strange to hear Tori of all people say that.

"You never again …?"

"Couldn't. Miscarriage took care of that for good."

Jax registered her tone as something not quite wistful, but like something one assumes when talking of road not taken. He also felt an enormous amount of relief, much to his shame. Safe, he was safe, he dodged another bullet. He never thought that way about sex before Maggie dropped the pregnancy boulder on him. Now no amount of precaution seemed enough, statistics be damned.

Out loud he opted for, "Oh. Shit. Did you…want to?"

"No. No," Tori said after a beat. "I don't think I ever want to make those choices again."

"I can't picture you as a mom," he said honestly and instantly regretted it.

"I can't picture you as a dad," she retorted, though not unkindly.

"Yeah, neither can anyone else, except for Maggie, apparently."

"That's your baby mama?"

Jax nodded. "We weren't together, nothing like that, it was just a condom snafu."

"Well, that's one epic origin story for your kid."

They laughed.

"What's its name, anyway?"

"Jeffrey."

"Seriously?"

"Yep."

"Alrighty then."

Tori reached for the bottled water on her nightstand and half-drained it before handing the rest to Jax.

"I'm going to kick you out soon. I sleep better alone as you might remember. But I thought maybe we could go for another round first?"

Jax took her mischievously raised eyebrow at its challenge.

"Rising for the occasion as we speak, chief."

"You goofball." She laughed, hitting him with a pillow. Then they got to business.

On his way out, Jax looked over the framed prints of the famous or semi-famous people Tori had worked on. One caught his eye, and he paused. The similarity was undeniable, but it made no sense. No logical sense whatsoever.

Jax got to his house very late or, technically, very early. He figured he was going to be tired anyway, so why did it matter if he took a long way home. The town was peaceful at night—a completely different energy all around. He looked up wishing he could see more stars, but light pollution took care of that pretty thoroughly. A song started forming in his head—that's how they always came to him, unbidden and unexpected, sometimes just a line or a chord progression. A tease, a sliver, a glimpse of a song to come, a story to tell. This one was melancholy, something in G minor, a soulful elegy of bygone days. His fingers moved as if his guitar was right there. The night welcomed his melody.

Or maybe that wasn't quite right. It *was* melodic, but

there was a discordant quality to it too; the strange unease in the way it flowed. Jax searched his mind—no longer drunk just temporarily oxytocin-elated—for its origin. It was only when he was standing on his front porch, looking for his keys that he remembered where those chords came from.

"Jax, hon, is that you?"

"No, ma, it's George Clooney. He decided life with Amal and the twins was just too glamourous and wanted to settle down with someone more, you know, real."

"Very funny, hon. You just getting in?"

Jax didn't know why these conversations needed to take place—in raised voices to overcome the distance—when they were going to be sharing the same space in a minute, the minute it took him to take off his shoes and unload his pocket detritus on the entryway table.

He made his way into the kitchen, quiet in his stocking feet and bleary from the lack of sleep.

"Late night?" His mom wiggled her eyebrows suggestively at him, which looked admittedly hilarious. But she did take pity on him and poured him a strong cup of coffee.

"Hung out with Tori."

"How old is Tori?" His mom tried for a casual tone to mask her disapproval.

"Old enough, Mom," said Jax noncommittally. "Why are you up?"

"Jeffrey couldn't sleep. And then, I couldn't."

"Shit, he's still here?"

"Lower your voice, Jax. If you wake him after the night we had, I just might kill you."

"Why is he still here?" Jax whispered.

"Because Maggie asked me to look after him, and because he's my grandson, and because I love him. Is that good enough for you?"

"Sure. Sure." He raised his hands in the international 'I'm good, you're good, we're good' sign of surrender.

"Maggie's coming to get him early. Her new job is shift work, all over the place."

Jax nodded. Sipped the bitter brew in his cup.

"You working today, hon?"

"Yep."

"Better load up on that coffee then."

"Yeah, I'll grab a shower, maybe squeeze a quick nap in before I have to head out. I got a couple of hours still."

"I was just going to ask if you wanted to give Jeffrey his breakfast."

"Pass, ma, too tired."

His mom tutted disapprovingly. "The baby will forget he has a dad at this rate, Jax."

"The baby doesn't know he has a dad. The baby knows nothing yet. Wonderfully blissed-out state of perfect ignorance."

That got him a reproving headshake. "I just wish you were more…"

"Fatherly?"

"Involved." His mom, ever so tactful.

"I changed my entire life around to pay for this kid, that's

plenty involved."

"Wasn't what I meant, hon."

"I gotta go if I want to grab that nap, ma. Thanks for the

coffee." Jax kissed her on the cheek and went downstairs to

his basement den.

The shower beat down on his muscles like a much-needed

massage, but afterward, sleep wouldn't come. He was never

much of a napper. Jax picked up his guitar—a far cry from

Mr. Chambers' Martin I—and strummed it, letting his fingers

do their thing, letting his mind recollect the melody that had

come to him earlier. He knew only a few perfect things in this

life, but playing music was one of them. The way it felt—so

pure, so organic, like a part of him, a natural extension of him;

the way it allowed him to express himself and the thoughts

that often resisted being put into words alone.

The calluses on his left-hand fingers welcomed the tautness of the strings. It had been too long since he'd played simply for pleasure. He sped up, starting with G minor, letting the chord progressions come to him naturally and take him where they would. The soulfulness of Bs, the somber tones of As. The melody was almost fully formed…when the baby's wail ripped through the fabric of the predawn silence upstairs.

He didn't think he was playing that loudly, not enough to wake the kid. It probably had nothing to do with him; much like he wished none of it did.

Jax put his guitar down, leaning it against the wooden arm of the futon, and reached for his headphones, clamping them down over his ears. Some rock star he was. He plugged his headphones into his phone and scrolled down his music list to select a band, one of his all-time favorites, one that had been on his mind a lot lately. *Now that's music*, he thought, closing his eyes. *That's music.*

Nothing like doing a job you already hate on no sleep. No amount of coffee could help with that. And no amount of coffee, on any day, could make talking to Donna Collodi tolerable.

This time she was going on about her new fad diet—and there had been many. Jax let her carry on for a while, since he simply had no energy to protest. Donna was in rare form, or maybe just hungry. All those diets, he reasoned, had to take a toll.

She didn't need to diet, not that he could tell. She wasn't overweight by any means and appeared fit for her age and sprightly. Maybe it was just about control.

Jax idly studied her face as she talked, figuring it ought to pass for eye contact in a pinch. Donna's face was composed of wrinkles, small bright eyes, a huge nose, and a motormouth beneath it and surrounded by a halo of thick dyed blonde wavy hair. The overall effect and the energy she put out made it nearly impossible to guess her exact age. It had to be somewhere on the south side of the midway point, but likely before the retirement cutoff.

He thought about cleaning toilets—the next item on his daily agenda—and wondered if that might be preferable to hearing this tiny woman extoll the virtues of the paleo diet.

"So, the idea is to model your diet on the diet of people whose life expectancy was approximately twenty years, right?" *Shit, he didn't mean to say it out loud.* Donna didn't react well to sarcasm. Fortunately, she seldom recognized it either.

She paused for a second at his interjection, like he inputted some unrecognizable data into her programing that sent her OS twitching, and then resumed as if nothing happened. Oh well, he thought, at least he was getting paid for this, technically.

Eventually, he was released from Donna's web to find that cleaning toilets was indeed preferable, at least on that day with his brain fuzzy from sleep deprivation. At least, it was quiet.

Nothing but the watery slaps of the mop, the silent gliding of the Lysoled paper towels across the surfaces. And the low hum of his thoughts slowly ramping up into something louder and more insistent. Sometimes he just wanted to ease the pressure of it, to have someone to talk to, someone who'd listen.

He talked all day, it seemed. At work with Donna or clients or co-workers, at home with his mon…but it wasn't the same. Not like talking to Deek or Tori. He craved more than a perfunctory exchange of words. Or maybe just something different.

After lunch, he decided to check in on Mr. Chambers. The old guy never had any visitors, as far as Jax could remember. It was sad, really.

"Hi, Mr. Chambers. Remember me? I'm Jax. I work here."

The old man's eyes swam over Jax's face, unfocused.

"I was wondering if maybe I could talk to you. Ask you a couple of questions. About your tattoos. About your guitar."

Mr. Chambers remained silent, but Jax thought he saw a small muscle twitch in his craggy face. He took it as an encouraging sign.

"See, I'm a musician too. I play guitar too. Nothing as nice as your Martin, just a pawn-shop Ibanez. And I'll tell you, that took ages to save up for."

Jax paused, waiting…hoping for something. There was nothing so far. He couldn't tell how trapped inside his mind the old man was, really. He didn't know if even the experts could. The mind was a mysterious place.

"I'm in a band. I mean, well, I was in the band. Not anymore. They replaced me. I don't even play much anymore, but the other day, you were humming this melody and it's been haunting me ever since. I tried playing it …"

At this, there was a reaction at last. The old man turned to Jax, locked eyes with his, and shook his head, quite firmly. He reached out his age-gnarled hand to grasp Jax's wrist.

"No," he whispered. "Don't."

Jax startled, repelling inwardly from the spidery bony fingers, but steeling himself not to move. "I don't mean to steal your ideas. I'm all about intellectual property. I've just…I had this crazy idea. See, coming up, my favorite band was Dreadnought. Their frontman was my idol. And then he disappeared, the band split up, and that was that. Anyway, I know this is going to sound kind of crazy, but this guy, he was heavily inked and his tattoos, well, they look a lot like yours. See, I know this tattoo artist, and she's the one who did them. She's got photos I saw, and I know, *I know* it makes no sense, because of your age and all, but I was just wondering if maybe you knew him. Chase?"

The old man was silent. A tear quietly formed and inched its way out of the corner of his eye, sliding down along one of the many vertical wrinkle tracks of his face.

"I don't mean to upset you, Mr. Chambers. Believe me. It's just that you have the same guitar and the same tattoos, and I mean, I know you're not him. You're, like, old enough to be his dad, at least. But I just can't figure it out, it's like a puzzle. It's just so strange."

Another tear. More silence.

"OK." Jax lifted his hands in surrender. "I'll go. I'm sorry. I really didn't mean to upset you. I think … it's just my own crap all coming up, muddling my brain. I get that a person shouldn't bring their personal life to work, but it doesn't just disappear when I enter the Cherry Orchard, you know. I wish it did. And I'm sorry to unload it all on you. That's shitty. I apologize. I have, you know, I have people in my life, I just can't talk to them about things, not always. Cause they're happy, and I'm stuck. It's like life comes easy to them, and I feel like I'm forced to row against the current the entire way. I got a kid I don't know how to love, a job I hate, a band I love and no longer play in. I'm just kinda lost, you know."

Jax shut his mouth and looked around in horror. He had no idea coming in here that he was going to say all these things. In a way, Mr. Chambers made an ideal listener, but there was something horrifying, almost abusive, about vomiting up all his personal crap like that on someone who was essentially a perfect stranger. Jax never cared for psychoanalysis—derided the concept, in fact—and here he was, imposing an impromptu talk-therapy session upon a helpless old man. Shit. So much for quiet, dignified forbearance. He was worse than Donna. Jax hung his head in shame.

"You can have it." The voice was so quiet, Jax thought he might have hallucinated it. "You can have the guitar."

He *does* talk, was Jax's first thought. His second thought was, WHAT? No way! Things like that just didn't happen in real life. The lottery ticket of one's days got scratched every day and left one wanting. Sooner or later, you came to expect the unmatched numbers, the small casual failures, the slowly crushing indifference of existence. It was almost easier to accept that than a sudden win.

"Just—" The old man paused, as if unused to so many words. "Just play me something."

And so Jax took the Martin, strummed it a few times, and then played a quick tune by The Smiths.

"More."

Jax did a Beatles medley.

"One of yours," Mr. Chambers wheezed quietly.

Jax paused for a beat, then launched into his band's greatest hit, "Young and Stupid", their age-defying anthem.

He thought he spied a ghost of a smile on the old man's face. Emboldened, he strummed the intro to Dreadnought's "Stardust Junkie." And then, he played the entire song, his fingers calling up the chord progressions from memory, retrieving them from where they were permanently embedded into the vast record library of his mind.

"I love that song," he said, smiling, shaking his head as he let the final chord ring out. "That was the first Dreadnought song I ever heard. The first one I ever learned to play."

The old man brought a shaking hand to his lips. There was an expression in his eyes, something almost rapturous, like a great memory relived. It was a while before he spoke again.

"It only took a day to write. A week to record. The

producers wanted to change the lyrics in the chorus, but we didn't let them. The radios tried to ban it—the word junkie rubbed everyone the wrong way, those were the times, but in the end, it went platinum."

"Yeah, yes, I know." Jax nodded emphatically. He'd heard it all, watched the three-hour all-inclusive documentary on Dreadnought so many times. It took a moment to register that Mr. Chambers said *we*. And that was the time that Donna chose to page him to the lobby. ASAP, her canned voice demanded, somehow throwing her grating accent on each of the four letters of the abbreviation. *Ah, His Master's Voice*, Jax remembered the old RCA commercial, bitterly. He put the Martin down and made his excuses. It would take a while to process what had just happened, maybe later, when he came back for his new guitar. Maybe then. For now, with a full heart and a mind swimming, off he went.

In 1916 (or 1917, depending on the source), American Guitar Manufacturer C. F. Martin and Co. designed a very special acoustic guitar. It had been copied frequently since, but they were the first. The difference was the body's size, hence the name—dreadnought.

At the time, a dreadnought was a large battleship, so this was one good-sized guitar, much larger than most, providing it with a robust and resonant tone. These instruments became known as D-size guitars, or, colloquially, as dreads. The higher the number following the D, the more decorative ornamentation on the body of the instrument. Which made D-28 a thing of beauty all around. A guitar with a sound so iconic, so popular, that at one point in the 1950s you'd have to wait a year or two just to get your hands on one. It became closely associated with the sound of bluegrass, but you could do whatever you wanted with it, whatever your talent and imagination would allow. Anyone who's anyone in music had played this baby. Alphabetically, we're talking Cash, Clapton, Dylan, Garcia, Lennon, McCartney, Page, Presley, Mitchell, Williams, Young. And that's just for starters.

And then, there was Aaron Chase. The man who blazed onto the music scene with the brightness of a sungrazer comet. Or maybe more of a supernova. Whoosh. Mesmerizing, impossible to ignore. Aaron Chase and his band, The Dreadnought, were well poised to redefine the modern music scene. Everyone said so. Their music defied classification, it roared from heavy metal to classic rock, every so often slowing down into something close to old-school country or the blues.

It was almost as if they knew their time was limited and wanted to do it all, there was a certain voracious hunger that drove them. A devil-may-care attitude that defined them, and yet it made everyone care; made everyone stand up and listen. Or so it seemed at the time. The way you discover a band when you're young, and it becomes your entire world.

That's how it was for Jax and Deek and their friends back then. Dreadnought was THE BAND. The band they loved, the band they most wanted to be like. The fact that the guys were local was the ultimate cherry on top.

At the time, they were too young to know the history of the beautiful guitar Chase played or understand the name of the band. It had 'dread' in it and that was enough. Kickass status was a thing easily bestowed back in those days, when things were simpler.

Dreadnought provided the soundtrack to their misspent youth. It spoke to their anger, their bewilderment at the world they were rapidly growing up into, their frustrations.

And then, one day it was over. Just like that. Aaron Chase disappeared. Vanished into proverbial thin air. At the height of his fame, with everything going for him, riding high on the fresh release of his first solo track— a devastating ballad of wanting more, of a powerful yearning for things beyond one's grasp—a stylistic and tonal departure that seemed to resonate with everyone no matter what side of the musical fence they grazed on.

Jax could still remember the music video for that track. Barebones, clean aesthetics, four walls, and a chair. A small window. Chase sitting on a plain wooden chair with his trusty Martin D-28, the two of them as one. His long hair is tied back, his face is rocking his trademark beard. His blue eyes are tracking the daylight's trajectory as it slowly dies into darkness, and Chase is just playing and singing his heart out.

Jax, who had always loved music, couldn't remember ever being moved by a song quite as much. He felt it in his very bones, it aligned with something fundamental within his being. Try as he might to emulate it over the years, it never came out the same. Not even when Deek, an objectively better performer, gave it a shot later. They knew the lyrics, knew the chords, but it just didn't sound right, not like it did when Aaron Chase sang it.

No one could explain the disappearance. No one could solve it. No one was even sure there was something worth solving there. Perhaps, it was merely a case of a popular musician walking away from it all at the height of his game. Getting out while the getting was good. Perhaps his last song was a goodbye note to his fans, to the world. Perhaps he was living out his days in anonymous comfort on some tropical island or, more to his style, in a rugged Thoreauvian manner of wooded privacy.

Either way, the man was gone. Speculation abounded, but eventually, died down. The rest of the band didn't even try to carry on afterward. They knew their heart was cut out, and without it, there would be no point. They went on to join or form their own, less successful bands. Dreadnought became a thing of legend. And, like most legends, immortal.

All of this was public knowledge. For some, a mere VH1 Behind the Music episode, for others, so much more. Jax was in the latter camp, so was Deek. That's why Deek was looking at him so intently right now. Because the story Jax was spinning was simply too wild to be believed.

"So, wait. You didn't take the Martin?" Deek sounded incredulous.

"I wanted to, but I was afraid Donna would raise a stink about it. I'll figure it out, find a way."

"Is this about the other night?" Deek asked after a beat, looking down at his hands.

"What? The other…no, not about that."

"I'm sorry we had to replace you. I am. But you've been

busy, and we needed an extra guitar."

"He's good, the new guy," Jax said magnanimously.

"Yeah, he is." Deek nodded. "But he isn't you. He isn't one of us. Then dynamics are different."

"You're gonna talk about your chemistry, like it's some rom-com review?"

"Hardy, har, har." Deek took a long swig of his beer. "Look, bro, no hard feelings, right? It's just life. We just wanted to play. It's our thing. You gotta do your thing, I respect that. But you know, life goes on."

"I know." Jax nodded. "I get it."

"Really?" Deek squinted at him exaggeratedly, comically.

"Really."

Deek appeared relieved and shifted gears immediately, away from all the awkwardness. "I saw you left with Tori the other night. How was that?"

"Hot and heavy, like always."

"She's a wild one."

Jax wondered if Deek and Tori had ever…he wouldn't be surprised. The thought didn't faze him one way or another. His expectations were all adjusted accordingly in that arrangement.

"Did you know that Tori tattooed Aaron Chase back in the day?"

"No shit?"

"No shit."

"She told you?"

"Didn't have to. I saw the photos on her wall of fame."

Deek nodded appreciatively. "She never talks about it."

"Maybe there's a reason there. Maybe they were an item, and when he took off …"

"Yeah, maybe."

They paused for a while, listening to the Dreadnought record Jax specifically put on for this conversation. It sounded as good as ever, timeless, a true classic.

"So, you really think this old dude is Aaron Chase?"

Jax ran his hand through his hair. "I don't know what to think, to be honest."

"But he's old; he's like ancient, right? So, Chase would be what…pushing fifty now, tops? Not that old, at all. So, maybe this guy was just a crazy fan, copied his ink? Got his guitar?"

"But he had to have become a crazed fan in his, what, like, sixties, for that? Who'd tattoo a senior citizen like that?"

"Not Tori."

"No, likely not Tori."

Deek chewed his lip in thought. "Still, though, devils' advocate like, odds are against it. Logic's against it."

"Maybe he's got that … what's that …" Deek searched his memory. "Progeria shit. It ages a person rapidly."

They whipped out their phones and did some googling. It didn't seem to fit. It started within the first two years of children's lives.

"Well, maybe there's something like that for adults?"

More googling. Zero, zilch, nada.

"Would you just ask him?"

"I could. And he could lie."

"Why would he lie?"

"Because he's an old man at the end of his life with nothing to do and nowhere to go and no one to visit him. Why not?"

"You're a cynical bastard, Jax." Deek shook his head in mock seriousness.

"Yeah, well, you have your entire life upended by a faulty condom, and then talk to me about cynicism."

Deek laughed, almost spilling his beer. "Don't even joke like that, brother, don't even joke like that."

They talked more about other things; they drank more. It was as much fun as always to hang out, easy to overlook the fact that their lives were slowly and irrevocably drifting in different directions. Jax tried playing Deek the new song he was working on, but it was still missing that certain something. They improvised. It was almost but not enough to forget that they were no longer bandmates.

Eventually, Jax got too drunk to care and soon afterward, too drunk to make it home, so he crashed on Deek's couch as he had done so many times before.

The morning sun was much too bright for his liking. The sun never shined that brightly in his apparently ironically named daylight basement. Jax woke up and immediately felt the beers he consumed the night before.

He stumbled into the bathroom, emptied his bladder for what felt like half an hour, then washed his hands and face thoroughly. His reflection in the above-the-sink mirror told him it was going to take a lot more than that to get back to resembling a living person.

Jax angled himself toward the kitchen.

"Ah, the sleeping beauty awakes." Deek was one of those infuriating morning people, bright-eyed and bushy-tailed irrespective of what he got up to the night before. Then again, he did make coffee.

"Life juice, gimme." Jax zombie-shuffled toward the coffeemaker.

"No work today?"

"No work. Finally. I swear the time between the days off gets longer every week."

"*Oh, poblecito. Todo trabajo, no juega.*" Deek's housemate, Carmen, waltzed into the kitchen and started getting out the ingredients for an omelet. Carmen was born in the US and only knew Spanish because she was raised by her abuela who spoke no English.

Deek's grand idea, which had a lot to do with trying to alter their friendship into something more romantic, was that he should learn Spanish and Carmen should be the one to teach him. And so, for the sake of proper immersion, they tried to only speak Spanish to each other at home. Every time Jax came over, he struggled to keep up.

"Te quedas a desayunar?" Carmen asked him.

His fuzzy brain picked out the word for breakfast, making him nod enthusiastically.

"Huevos?"

Oh wait, he knew this. "Cualquier cosa."

Deek laughed. "You're butchering the pronunciation, dude."

"Well, we don't all have a live-in teacher," Jax replied with a shrug. You had to pity Deek and his ongoing pursuit of Carmen, who was quite obviously playing for the other team. It took a massive amount of hope and denial to persevere the way Deek did. He was telling himself Carmen was probably bi, but hey, at the very least he'd come out bilingual out of this arrangement. Plus, the girl was a great cook. A heavy hand on spices, but her abuela taught her well. El desayuno at Deek and Carmen's was to die for.

Later, Jax left them to their companiably bickering selves

and went for a long walk. In the broad daylight, it seemed crazy to imagine that an old man living out his last days at the Cherry Orchard was his favorite rock star, gone all these years. Like the sort of wishful thinking a kid might indulge in. A treasure map with an X on it. What he had to do was apologize to Mr. Chambers and leave him alone. He had embarrassed himself enough.

People came to the Cherry Orchard for peace and quiet. He ought to respect that. They didn't care if his life didn't go to plan; they've had their own, that—planned or otherwise—were in their twilight now and they didn't need his drama.

Jax still didn't feel like an adult, but he knew he was no longer a kid, and the time had come for him to put away childish things. The irony of knowing this quote from *Ghost in the Shell* anime and not from the bible didn't even occur to him.

The sound that greeted him upon entering his house was a wail. Again. He had long given up on discerning whether Jeffrey's wails were of happiness or discomfort. His mom swore there was a difference and if Jax would just spend more time with his kid, he'd know it too.

But then, he didn't want to spend any more time with the kid, and she always seemed happy to, so why ruin a perfect balance? Was he supposed to feel guilty about it? Because he didn't, really. Most days he was simply too tired and weary for feelings as layered and heavy as guilt. Besides, wasn't it costing him enough already?

The wail raked his ears like nails on a chalkboard. Jax took a chance on presuming this one was a happy one and poked his head in the living room, where the baby and his grandma were playing on the couch.

"Hi, hon. Out all night again?"

"Just at Deek's. Nothing too wild."

"You eat?"

"Yep. Had one of Carmen's fire-on-the-plate specials."

"Well, so long as it doesn't turn into fire-in-you-know-where later." Jax's mother's idea of spicy food was using an extra dash of black pepper.

"It'll be worth it."

"Gross. Come play with Jeffie." Jeffie, Jax thought, was an even worse moniker somehow.

He reluctantly joined them on the couch and patted the baby's back gingerly.

"Come on. Take him." With this, she practically shoved the kid at Jax, so that he had no alternative but to make some sort of a nest out of his arms. The baby's heaviness always took him by surprise—it was so … substantial. Like an anchor, his lizard brain whispered in the dark, like your anchor. Like a deadweight pulling you down.

Jax shook his head and tried to focus on the kid. "Did he get more hair, ma?"

"He's getting more hair every day. Going to have a beautiful head of hair just like his daddy."

Jax did indeed have nice hair—rock star hair that required no product to maintain that sexy bedhead look. It saved time on grooming. Whatever connotations his appearance had with bed were authentically earned—he was frequently sleepy-eyed and messy-haired as a side effect of not spending enough time between the sheets, but no one needed to know that. Overall, he was happy enough with his looks. It was the rest of his life that needed improvement.

He tried picturing the baby as an adult, looked for familiar features becoming more prominent, thought of the kid reaching his full height of six feet, but in the end, Jax's imagination just wouldn't stretch that far. He wondered what the baby saw when he looked at him. Couldn't have been pleasant, he was sure, since the wailing resumed, and this time it was definitely on the upset side of things.

"What'd you do?" His mother came back from the kitchen. "I barely made it through half a sink of dishes, and he's crying his head off."

"Nothing, ma, nothing. The kid just hates me."

"No, he doesn't," she said in that gooey baby voice and, putting the dish towel down, reached for Jeffrey. "Jeffie loves his daddy."

Jeffie paused as if cognizant of being talked about, sighed a funny deep oddly adult-like sigh, and puked on Jax's shirt.

"Better out than in, kiddo." Jax's mom beamed at the kid like he had just recited the alphabet, affectionately patting Jeffrey's back.

"Is it?" Jax studied the warm greenish puddle redecorating his vintage concert T-shirt.

"Take it off and presoak it before tossing it into the

laundry," she said over her shoulder, taking the baby back to the kitchen with her.

Jax sat there for a second, marveling at how naturally she took to grandmothering—it *had* to have been genetic. Otherwise, why would she want to put herself through all the motions she already went through years ago—with presumably more energy and zeal—with her own son. Was she just looking for something else since then to pour her love and time into?

His mom won a lawsuit years ago, one of those stupid things you read about on the news and shake your head at…like, how did you *not* think a hot coffee was hot? Well, she did it. A random stroke of fortune of meeting the right lawyer at the right time, a lawyer in the aftermath of their win had introduced her to a savvy financial advisor. As a result, she didn't have to work, provided she lived modestly. Their house was long-ago paid off by her long-dead parents. Outside of occasional side projects for her former employer, she had a lot of free time. Maggie was taking advantage of that, but no one but Jax saw it that way. And what did he know, really? Everyone seemed to be happy but him.

Jax made his way to his basement lair. The murky light down there was just enough not to walk his shins into furniture corners. He took off his shirt and rinsed it in the sink. Then put some detergent on it, rubbed it in, and left it sitting there.

He'd hate to see the shirt ruined—he remembered the day he got it so vividly. Deek had just gotten his license and finally inherited his old man's gas-guzzling beater. They drove to the concert with the windows down, blasting their music on the stereo that threatened to give out the entire way, crackling and straining to accommodate their passion for bass.

Jax remembered the concert, too. Sweaty bodies smelling of cheap beer and pot, mashing together to the music; the beat you could feel in your bones. The elation they felt afterward.

They almost crashed the car on the way home, but none of it mattered. Being close to death for a moment only made them feel more alive. That was it, wasn't it? He *felt* so alive back then. And now … now he just *was* alive.

His heart pumped blood around his body, his brain fired neurons, his body carried on with the motions of quotidian life. But the spark was gone, wasn't it?

He thought he must be too young to feel that way. Not even thirty. His idols had accomplished so much by the time they were his age. And Jax…Jax had a list of failures to his name. A failed musician, a failed son, a failed father, a failed condom user for crying out loud.

Is this what life was going to be like from now on, he wondered—a series of disappointments, a chain of nothingness? A dead-end job, a wailing kid, a cash-hungry ex, a poorly lit basement with beat-up furniture for a home. A life of proverbial quiet desperation with no power, no agency, no excitement—nothing to show for it.

Jax suddenly had a very clear image of his future and the bleakness of it took his breath away.

He stood up and stretched, rubbed his hands over his face, and then pushed his fingers through his hair. This had to be how depression won the day. He knew he had to do something, so he picked up his guitar and tried bringing to life the song that haunted his mind.

Some chords here and there sounded right, but overall, the melody stubbornly refused to flesh itself out. Jax tried losing himself in the music the way he used to, surrendering to the sheer power of creating a sound out of nothingness, the pleasure of shaping the silence to sing to you, and it worked for a while…until more noise from upstairs came through and ripped straight through the gossamer-thin solace he had fashioned for himself.

He sighed and sat his guitar down. Finished rinsing the shirt, squeezed the water out, and hung it up on the shower curtain rod. Didn't have the heart to check if the stain set.

Instead, he found another clean-enough-smelling T-shirt, put

it on, and headed out.

It was an unseasonably nice day. The kind that makes cynics ponder global warming and optimists go out and carpe diem. Jax shrugged off his hoodie as the sun and the brisk pace of his walk warmed him up. He paid no attention to where he was going, trying simply to shake off the dark cloud that descended upon him at home and appeared determined to follow him around. It reminded him of an anti-depressant commercial he'd seen a long time ago. In it, the animated dark cloud was dispelled quite easily with a few extra chemicals. Jax wasn't against it, on principle, it seemed more effective than talking things out. In fact, he was pretty sure his mom took them now and again—something had to be responsible for all that relentless positivity—but didn't think it would be right for him.

Jax looked around. There were people everywhere, enjoying the weather, enjoying their lives. Sometimes he had difficulty thinking of strangers the way he thought about himself or people he knew—each a narrator in their own story. Is that what compassion was? Jax had recently learned a new word—*sonder*. One of those awesome foreign words for emotions and feelings that English simply didn't have, like *schadenfreude* or *saudade*. *Sonder* meant something like a gained awareness of others as individuals with their own struggles. He couldn't remember what language it that was from, but he liked it. Even if it highlighted a shortcoming of his.

Would life be different if he viewed Maggie as a flawed and complex person with her own challenges and not as merely the villain of his story? Probably. But how would he even do that—change his mind like that?

Jax had no answers, but all that walking was making him

hungry. He stopped at a hot dog stand and grabbed one with everything. Ate it on the bench nearby and came back for another. Washed it all down with a bottle of water, because pouring a chemically laced brew of cola down the questionably sourced meat product just seemed wrong, even by his lax dietary standards.

Afterward, looking around, Jax noticed that he was in Tori's neighborhood. Consciously or subconsciously, his feet had carried him there, so he figured he should just come in and say hi.

There was a large man in the chair getting his gigantic bicep inked up. The guy was obviously too testosterone-laden to whimper, but every so often he grunted. His ZZ-Top beard was glistening with sweat.

"Hey stranger," said Tori, taking a pause just long enough to look up. "What brings you by? Finally decided to get some color on that pasty virgin canvas of yours?"

Now that he was here, he had an idea. It did indeed have to do with ink, but not with getting any on or in his skin. Specifically, it had to do with another man's body art, a matter Jax not too long ago had vowed to himself to leave alone. Just a couple of questions, he told himself now, no harm in that, just a couple of quick questions.

"Nah, not today. Thought we could have a coffee maybe?"

"Sure, take a seat, I'll be done here in about twenty."

Jax took a seat on one of the retro vinyl chairs that lined the longer of the walls. It was, he realized the first time he'd ever been in the parlor. He'd been upstairs a few times, sure, but never down here. He was probably the only one of his friends without any ink.

It was a nice place. Though nice probably wasn't the right world. It suited Tori; like her apartment, it reflected her personality and showcased the work she's done. Lots of red, again. Must be her color. More photos of former clients lined the walls. A few local celebrities. No Chase.

There was a coffee table creatively fashioned out of wooden crates and covered in magazines. Unsurprisingly, most of them were about tattoos, but there was a not-too-old issue of *Rolling Stone* that he found of interest.

Twenty minutes of manly grunts later, the bearded giant departed. Jax put the magazine back down on the pile and got up.

"So." Tori smiled at him uncertainly.

"So." He smiled back.

"Didn't think I'd see you again so soon. Guess you just woke up overwhelmed with a burning desire to share some java with me?"

"And to ask you a question."

"Ah, okay, there it is. Well, at least you're honest. We can skip the coffee; I got the next appointment in fifteen. Just ask what you came to ask and drop me off a large soy latte later."

Funny, Jax thought, I would have pictured her for a straight black kinda gal.

"So, the other day," he started, "I saw a photo on your wall. In your apartment. I wasn't snooping, it was just there, and I noticed it on the way out. It had you and Aaron Chase on it."

She nodded, narrowing her eyes as if to say, Yeah and? Ever so slightly defensive, Jax thought.

"Well, he was my idol coming up. All of us, we were obsessed with him. Dreadnought to this day is my favorite band, and Chase's last song to this day is my favorite song."

"Yeah, he was good," Tori allowed quietly, wistfully.

"So, I mean, I didn't know you knew him."

"Knew him. Inked him."

"What … what was he like?"

"What was he *like*, Jax? What sort of a question is that? He was a man. As flawed and angry and messed up as the rest of us. Haven't you ever heard that saying about how you should never meet your heroes? I think it's the same for trying to get to know them posthumously. The idea is that you're inevitably going to be disappointed."

"I won't be."

She shook her head and smiled an exasperated smile. At that moment she looked more beautiful and older than he had ever seen her. Somewhere beneath that devil-may-care attitude and dyed hair and loud makeup was a woman in her 40s with experiences and wear and tear of life to match. Tori was her own portrait in the attic.

"He had this innate sense of destiny," she said after a beat. "He wouldn't allow things to get in the way of that. Aaron would do whatever it takes, pay whatever cost there was to get to where he wanted to get to. Very…very single-minded, driven. Obsessive, even."

"Sounds intense."

"You have no idea."

Jax paused, unsure of how to ask the next thing. Sometimes, there were no right words and you just had to go for it.

"So, were you guys like hanging out, or did you just do his ink?"

"Pry much?" She cocked her eyebrow at him, a signature Tori move.

"It's been so long, I figured it was safe. Like statute of limitations of something."

"We hung out some," she allowed vaguely.

"Must have been tough to be with someone like that."

"It was," Tori admitted, quietly.

Jax sensed he was upsetting her and tried shifting gears.

"Where'd he get this from, you think? This destiny thing?"

"You'll laugh, but he had this birthmark on his lower back that he was convinced looked like a guitar. And so, he always said he was predestined for rock'n'roll stardom. From birth."

"Did it really? Look like a guitar, I mean?"

"From the right angle, if you squinted at it, sure."

They shared a smile.

"Look, Jax, truth is, someone like Aaron, he didn't need a birthmark. If he didn't have it, he'd have seen a meaningful cloud shape and interpreted it his way. It was like he just *knew*, and the rest was pure confirmation bias."

"He knew he was going to be great." Jax nodded.

"Nah, you're misremembering, you were just a kid back then. He wasn't great to begin with, not always. He was good, really good, but great…that came later. His last song, now *that* was great."

Jax thought about it and could see the validity of Tori's point. He loved Dreadnought with the all-forgiving passion of youth; the nostalgia factor was difficult to override or take out of the equation completely. Dreadnought was the embodiment of all his hopes and dreams—the local boys made good, the local band playing on national radio, the local faces on MTV. But objectively speaking, it was possible they weren't the greatest band that ever lived. He allowed that without feeling like a traitor. That last song, though—pure genius.

"So, what changed? What took him from good to great, you think?"

Tori sighed. "That I don't know, Jax. He was getting all these crazy ideas then. Like he wasn't doing enough, he wasn't good enough. He started pushing himself, getting messed up, and looking for answers in strange places. Some seriously esoteric shit I didn't even want to go near."

"Oh. Like what?"

"Like that pentagram I inked on his stomach. Like that."

"Shit."

"Yeah, shit. But him and I, we were just about done by then anyway."

"Cause he was too intense?" Jax nodded in what he

thought was an understanding manner.

"No, Jax, it was because I got pregnant and I was afraid to bring a baby into the world, afraid to bring a baby into *his* world."

"Oh." Jax tried getting his foot out of his mouth, but it was stuck rather firmly.

"And then I miscarried and found Aaron on the bathroom floor collecting my blood and that was the end of that."

"Shit." Jax had exhaled the word. What did anyone say to that? What would have been a more eloquent way to express the sheer horror of it? And, beneath it all—beneath the nightmare's slick stygian surface—Jax clocked a strobe light-bright fascination that made him feel deeply, profoundly ashamed.

"I'm sorry," he added, remembering himself. He got the impression Tori didn't go around sharing personal details of her life all that often. Especially, things like that. "I'm so sorry you went through that."

Her shutters were already lowering themselves back down. "Live and learn," she said, shrugging, returning to her stoic self. "What sort of a parent would I have made anyway?"

"Probably a better one than me."

She quirked her head to the side, giving him a sympathetic look. "Still not vibing with the junior?"

"He puked on me this morning, does that count?"

"If there's one thing I learned from hanging out with rock stars and making grown men cry with my tattoo gun is that puking almost certainly equates to true love."

"Ha." You had to laugh. You had to appreciate this woman.

"Don't look so glum, sad boy. Things change."

"For the better?"

Tori gestured vaguely. "Sometimes. Maybe."

"I can't stop feeling like I fucked it all up. My life, my dreams …"

Tori thought about it for a moment. "I have this client. A

writer. Big thinker, big talker, this guy, never shuts up when he's getting work done. To hear him tell it, people get hung up on being heroes of their own stories. When in reality, it's way more complicated and way less exciting than that."

"What if I'm a villain of mine?"

"That's the thing. According to my client, anyway. No one ever is. Even if you don't think yourself a particularly compelling or sympathetic protagonist, you're still never the villain. Apparently, it's goes against our wiring, because to our own selves we are innately justifiable."

Jax scratched his chin. "That's pretty deep."

"Sure is." Tori smiled a crooked smile at him. "Think it over and cheer up."

"Thought you were into sad boys?"

"Yeah, yeah." She gave him a firm but gentle shove. "My appointment is here."

She nodded at the figure approaching the parlor's entrance. "You better scramble."

"I'll be back with your fancy latte as soon as I find the nearest coffee shop."

"You better," she said playfully, pushing him out.

After getting Tori a cringingly expensive latte from a nearby coffee shop, Jax found himself wandering aimlessly, thinking over the conversation he'd just had.

If not for Mr. Chambers and the mystery Jax saw or imagined there, he probably would have been devastated on some level. Intrigued and devastated—both. Did he want the mental image of his idol high as a kite scooping up the miscarriage blood of his girlfriend off the bathroom tiles? Well, no, of course not. But then, there *was* a certain morbid curiosity at play there too. What was Chase doing? What was he thinking? What next thrill was the man so aptly named chasing?

Jax knew all about the Satanic connections of some of the

musicians he had listened to over the years, especially of the heavy metal variety, but he'd always assumed it was mostly for show. Just like the over-the-top makeup and outrageous stage antics. They left it all behind when the spotlights were off, didn't they? They had to have. Who could sustain such a heightened state of madness for the duration?

Or maybe it stuck fast, the unshakeable conviction in one's immortality, in one's star trajectory. Maybe that's what killed.

Jax could never fall asleep after they performed, got too keyed up. He had to bring himself down with booze, gradually.

Strange, it felt like so long ago, and yet it wasn't, not at all. Feelings wreak havoc on time. Jax had childhood memories that were technicolor-vivid, and yet he sometimes struggled to recollect something as recent as last year's Thanksgiving.

Jax found himself near a park he recognized, one that had

recently undergone a major renovation, including a new playground and an addition of new trees and benches. It looked good, he had to admit, his tax money at work. The sort of place Jeffrey would be old enough for soon. He found a free bench— no easy task on a day that nice—and parked his weary bones for a while. From where he was sitting, he could clearly see the playground; all those happy kids and their parents looked just like a TV commercial: slightly exaggerated, slightly surreal. The entire scene, in fact, *the entire day* seemed to be dominated by a distinct uncanny valley vibe.

Jax wondered if Aaron Chase had ever sat like this, contemplating being a father. How he must have felt when Tori told him she was pregnant. How he must have felt when she lost the baby. Jax knew he wasn't good at that, imagining how others felt. Maggie had once accused him of lacking emotional intelligence, and he didn't disagree. He didn't even fire back that at least he didn't lack the actual intelligence. Or maybe he did. They had so many fights back then, before they settled into this uneasy détente for the kid's sake.

If Tori and Aaron's kid had lived, he'd be almost an adult now. With parents like that he would have probably turned out to be either the hippest cat that ever lived or, in some weird knee-jerk reaction of a role reversal, a total dweeb. Maybe Aaron would have lived too; maybe Tori would have become more of a prototypical mom. All these roads not taken.

Jax seldom speculated like this about Jeffrey. He knew he should, but despite the kid's discordant wails and off-color spit-ups, he never quite felt real to Jax. It was one of those things that can ring so true for a person but remain impossible to explain to others.

He tried to snap out of his spacing and found a woman on the next bench staring at him intently with something like disapproval veering on disgust. It took him a second to register that being a single man, alone, staring at a playground full of kids, might not have looked quite right from the outside. What a world, he thought, putting on his brightest, fakest smile for the woman before getting up and walking away.

Jax heard Maggie's voice as soon as he stepped into his house and seriously contemplated turning around and walking away. But he was tired, hungry and just maybe too mature at last for such a jerk move. He took off his shoes and padded into the kitchen. And there she was.

"Hiya, Jax. I'm just picking up Jeffie." She smiled at him, always extra nice in front of his mom.

"Hi, Maggie. Hi, Mom."

Maggie looked good; she always had the skill of letting well done hair and makeup turn average into cute. He didn't want to compliment her, though, never knowing what that could lead to. Besides, he didn't want to add any fuel to his mother's low-burning flame of hope that he and Maggie might end up properly getting together. All those romance novels she was always reading skewed her perspective of the real world.

"Molly tells me you had a day off."

"Yep."

"Didn't want to spend any of it with your kid?" *Ah, there it comes, the first stab.*

"No, Maggie, not really."

She never did deal with honesty well; it startled her each and every time. Maggie had worked customer service for so long that she lost the ability to separate genuine niceness from a fake one. One version or another, though, niceness was still her modus operandi.

"Jeffie would have loved some time with his daddy," she cooed strategically.

"Oh yeah, he told you that?"

"Not in so many words."

"Well, maybe when he starts communicating in actual words or something other than wails and puke, I'll reconsider. Good seeing you, Maggie. Later, kid." With that Jax made for the basement. He could practically hear the headshaking in his wake.

Jax microwaved a burrito while booting up his game system. He'd play his guitar later, he told himself, after his mind settled. He'd try to arrange the chords that haunted the back of his mind into something melodic, something coherent. He'd worry about the lyrics later; whatever he'd write now would be too shot-through with bitterness.

The burrito tasted vaguely like cardboard but not enough to merit getting up and checking the expiration date on the package. Food was food—he'd never been too picky. His taste buds discerned the difference between the deliciousness of Carmen's cooking and the blandness of cheap supermarket quick meals, but not enough to actively do something about it.

The game sucked him in with the same intensity that the real world used to spit him out. The bright action graphics and self-pity lulled Jax to sleep eventually. His guitar remained untouched.

"Jackson."

Donna's grating voice sliced through the morning calm. Jax made yet another mental note to never go to Brooklyn if that's how his name sounds there.

"Jackson, I have to talk to you. Can you come to my office?"

That sounded serious; serious enough to require discretion, which wasn't Donna's strong suit at the best of times. He told her he'd finish up the large window he was working on and meet her there. Maybe she expected him to follow her straight away like an obedient little soldier, but Jax knew if he abandoned the picture window halfway through, there would be streaks. The olds would have their view of the

Cherry Orchard streaked, and that wouldn't do. Not that he took any special pride in his work, but he figured so long as he was doing it, he might as well do it right. Plus, anything to delay spending time with Donna.

He finished up the window, all the while trying to imagine what Donna wanted to talk to him about. As unenthusiastic as he was about his job, he showed up on time and did the work. He was courteous with the clients. Polite to his coworkers. He couldn't think of a single thing he might have done wrong. Nevertheless, mild anxiety formed and began gnawing its way around at the bottom of his stomach.

"You wanted to see me?" Jax said redundantly, poking his head in. Donna's office was comfortable and tacky at the same time, a balancing act that took skill to manage. Overall, the space suited its master. There was even a framed poster of Brooklyn on the wall. She had to have missed the place, Jax thought, a place where everyone was so much more like her, or at least sounded like her.

"Come in, Jackson. Have a seat."

He did and he did. The cheap chair squeaked in protest but allowed it.

"How are you?" Jax said, playing for time. "How's the new diet?"

That took up at least a quarter of an hour and felt even longer than that, but at least it gave him some breathing room.

"Anyway," Donna cut herself off in a move unusual enough to attract the presses. "I received an unusual request from one of our clients."

"Oh." So, not a complaint then, Good, good.

"This client expressed explicit wishes to have you as their attendant."

"But I'm not …"

"I know, I know, you're just a janitor." The way she said it abraded Jax like the corset grade of sandpaper. "But the client insisted." The implication behind 'insisted' was 'paid'. The clients with enough money generally got whatever they wanted at the Cherry Orchard.

"So, I was thinking of a compromise. Maybe splitting up your hours between your custodial duties and your attendant ones. How would you feel about that?"

Jax prevaricated. "Who's the client?"

"Mr. Chambers." *Well, shit, way to bury the lede, Donna.*

"I'll do it," Jax said before his mind could offer him reasons not to. Sometimes it paid to go with one's gut.

"Good, great." She smiled, relaxing. He could tell Donna was a stickler, didn't like things upsetting her apple cart if she could help it.

"So, I'm thinking we do an even split. 50% janitorial work, 50% attendant. I must mention that attendant work pays more, so this'll be a mess for the admin to straighten out. But I'm sure they'll see you right. I'll let them know so they can get started on the paperwork."

"Okay, good. Thanks."

"As I'm sure you know, attendants have a lot of responsibilities and duties of their own. I'm going to have you shadow Alice for the day so that you get the idea."

"Today?"

"No time like the present," Donna replied, rearranging her wrinkles into a smile. In a home where people came to die, he supposed that was the truest of statements.

Alice was a heavyset Latina, surprisingly light on her feet for someone her size. Jax wondered if he should try out some of his half-assed Spanish on her but decided against it. Didn't want to overstep any boundaries of propriety or come across as too familiar.

There was a strong maternal vibe to Alice that really jelled with the clients she attended to. The olds were in so many respects like kids; there was something regressive about aging. The newly reacquired helplessness, the ever-increasing dependency on others.

Jax had never subscribed to the notion that old people inherently commanded respect. That made no sense to him. There were just people, like everyone else, only they've managed to stay alive longer. That's like saying the most respectable animals in the world should be turtles. Or whatever those immortal jellyfishes were.

He believed the elderly deserved more kindness and more help than others, but that was about it. In life, and especially at the Cherry, Jax had encountered enough of a variety of old people to know that they could be just as jerky or as rude or as racist as the rest of the world.

By the same logic, he didn't believe that movies, books, or albums should be considered classic just because they were old. Age did not denote quality in his mind.

That said, most of the people at the Cherry Orchard were actually pretty nice. Entitled, sure. This place wasn't cheap, and its clients carried themselves as people of privilege of any age are wont to do. But otherwise they were pretty nice.

Mr. Chambers wasn't an exception to that. He was more of an enigma.

He wanted Jax to get started right away, and so Jax did. Most of the old man's requests were simple enough, some of them were even fun. A Jim Jarmusch marathon was a pretty awesome idea. Jax was surprised someone that old would even know Jarmusch's work.

He was particularly struck by *Paterson*—the writer/director's arguably lesser movie. There was something about the way the main character moved through life with such quiet dignity, such stoic grace, that really spoke to Jax; he wished he could emulate the guy, be like him. Take life's curveballs as they came and persevere unscathed.

Real life was nothing like the movies, though. Real life's curveballs hit hard, pitting his soul like random asteroids, meteorites, and comets did the lunar surface. Maybe there was a song there, Jax wondered.

Outside of the assistance with quotidian tasks, the only thing Mr. Chambers had ever asked for was for Jax to play for him. The Martin was on offer anytime.

When Jax played that guitar, he got lost in the music. He thought the old man did too, judging by the peaceful expression that would come upon his face. Sometimes his fingers moved in time to Jax's, but they were so gnarled by age and arthritis, it was impossible to tell for sure.

They didn't talk much, the two of them, but they were building some sort of a rapport, Jax felt. Establishing a communication that didn't necessarily require words.

In that quiet room, cut off from the world by the excellent soundproof insulation the Cherry Orchard prided itself on, Jax's reality felt suspended somehow. Even his suspicions of the old man's connection to Chase seemed less important now, more distant.

It was a pleasant sensation, this temporary cessation of daily worries; like stepping out of time, getting off the train of life, and watching it go by without him for a while, knowing that he could jump back on at any time.

He wondered if that was how Mr. Chambers felt. And if it ever got to be too much. Maybe it did and that's why he, Jax, was here.

Sometimes, the old man would ask Jax about his life and listen. Really listen. Jax found himself unburdening more than he ever did, to anyone, and enjoying the strange elation that followed. There had been some good heart-to-hearts with Deek before, usually fueled by pot and booze, but he never had someone—a relative stranger at that —to just sit and listen to him. He didn't feel judged, he didn't feel challenged, he just felt…heard. After years of casual derision, Jax was finally beginning to understand the appeal of talk therapy. Only this was better and didn't cost him a penny.

In fact, he was making more money than before. Something he diligently avoided telling his mom or Maggie and hoped against hope that maybe Donna wouldn't blab to his mom either. He didn't want to risk his child support payments going up.

Jax's playing was improving too, he thought. He was getting more practice these days than he'd had in a long time. Funny to think, he'd be shining on stage now had he still been part of the band.

He saw the band play once more at Deek's invitation. They got some new material. He had to admit, begrudgingly, that the new guy was good, really good. Better than Jax, at least better than Jax of the last year, before he got replaced. Nowadays, they'd probably match up quite evenly.

He tried to let go of the bitterness and disappointment and just enjoy the music, but the feeling didn't really kick in until his third whiskey.

One of the band's new songs was particularly good. He tried playing it for Mr. Chambers the next day by memory. It sounded like something along the lines of what he'd been working on lately, on and off. Had the same wistful energy, reminiscent, in fact, of Chase's greatest hit. He played some of his own song too. The one that continued to elude him.

"I'm missing something," he admitted to the old man. "I know I am, but I can't put a finger on it. I just…I wanted to write a song that would break hearts, you know. Not just a thing to tap your feet and nod your head to, a track that burns brightly for a while and promptly disappears into the aether replaced by some new hotness, but a song that would genuinely resonate. Something that would stay with a person, light their darkness, give them solace. I don't know…" He ran his hand through his hair. "Crazy, right?"

"Not crazy at all. I get it." The old man spoke so

infrequently that it still tended to startle Jax.

"You ever ... you ever knew a song like that?" Sometimes Jax thought they talked *around* things too much. Jax —around his suspicions; the old man—around the truth. It was an unspoken agreement of sorts between them. A covenant of discretion.

"Kid, I was a song like that." *Well, there you go, said the believer to the cryptic.*

There were some attendant duties he enjoyed less, some genuinely unpalatable ones. To think, the guy who avoided changing his own kid's diaper, had to deal with adult shit. Shit that smelled distinctly worse and haunted your olfactory system like a gleefully malodorant ghost for hours afterward. Compared to that, bathing assistance was child's play.

Jax didn't notice the old man's birthmark straight away. He wasn't even sure he was looking for it, ambivalent as he was about this entire Chase thing. It was small enough to get

lost amid the ravages of time the old man's skin has endured.

Then one day, the light and the angle were just right and

there it was. And sure enough, if you squinted, it did look

just like a guitar.

In theory, Jax was a fan of denial. As a coping mechanism or as a life strategy it was pretty solid, all things considered. Until reality started messing with it.

Which was to say he was fine letting Mr. Chambers continue his Schrödinger-like existence of *is he or isn't he Chase* for the most part without questions. But the birthmark might have been too much. It jabbed at his psyche like the pea at the princess. The cognitive dissonance was beginning to overwhelm him.

Was he meant to go on pretending that Mr. Chambers was a feeble old man who merely shared body art and birthmarks with his ages-younger long-disappeared music idol or believe that Mr. Chambers was somehow Aaron Chase nearly aged into the ground before his time?

He could ask, he knew. He *should* just ask. There were no guarantees he'd receive a straight answer, but there was at least a chance that he might.

And then what, though?

Was he ready to live in a world strange enough to accommodate either of those revelations?

He was increasingly leaning toward a Yes.

Maybe, Jax thought, he was just lonely and looking for an obsession to take his mind off his mind. He'd been seeing less and less of Deek, who had finally found a Carmen doppelgänger that was willing to entertain him as a sexual partner and was making the most of it.

It would be exciting, he supposed, to find out the truth. If Mr. Chambers was indeed somehow Aaron Chase and he, Jax, was the only one to know it. What a rush that would be.

He almost asked so many times, the words poised right at the tip of his tongue and yet never making their way out.

Instead, he did his job and played the Martin, and slowly the old man had begun to give him pointers, small things here and there, chord change suggestions, tonal adjustments. Each one spot on.

Jax had never had a former teacher. All he knew he had picked up from YouTube and practicing. He found himself enjoying the arrangement, looking forward even to playing the old man something he had worked on the previous evening and getting his reaction.

He never quite got close to finishing the song, *his song*, though. It still sat in the corner of the record shelf of his mind, taunting him.

When he talked to Mr. Chambers about it and was asked to explain exactly what the problem was, he found it difficult to put into words. Whatever was missing was too elusive even to discuss.

"You strive for purity, for something perfectly melodic," said the old man thoughtfully after a while, "But perfect, as they say, is the enemy of good. Sometimes, you have to throw a spanner in the works. It may seem incongruous, it may seem discordant, but in the end, it's the saving grace."

Jax had thought about it. And thought about it some more. He relistened to Chase's last track with a critical ear, over and over, and there it was, the discordance the old man was talking about. He wondered how he had never noticed it before, but having heard it once, he heard it *every* time. A single unexpected chord change that rang out over the words *want*, *blaze*, and *live* in each of the three verses. So, *that's* what made it sing, *that's* what made it sizzle. He felt like someone who had uncovered a great secret and got to have it all to himself.

Not *The Secret,* that nonsense Donna was yammering on about for the first couple of months of his hiring, before moving on to the greener pastures of more recent fads, but something private, something … almost magical.

He began practicing more, experimenting more with different chord shapes and progressions, taking a bolder approach to his composition.

Mr. Chambers approved. He could tell by the Mona Lisa

smile that ghosted along the old man's features.

Time was passing faster now that he was busier, and the things he was busy with actually had value to him. Jeffrey got heavier and sprouted hair at long last, though he continued doing his best banshee impression whenever Jax tried to spend any time with him.

The kid was still spending an inordinate amount of time at their house, and Maggie was still politely and subtly bitching him out on his parenting skills every time she saw him, but it no longer carried the same sting now that he had his own world to flee to.

Funny, he'd always had his getaways, from a blanket fort as a kid to video games to music as he became older, but now it had taken on a new weight, acquired a different dimension. It wasn't just for fun, anymore— it was serious now. And seriously immersive. He could lose himself in his music for hours, letting the world outside and all its distractions just fade away. He wasn't happy, he knew. But he was occupied in a way that was the next best thing. Maybe the closest thing to happiness for someone like him. He was even beginning to imagine the future with something like hope. This music thing—what if he could take it further? He'd dreamt of it once, why not again? He played better than ever these days. And fame … well, fame if achieved, would change everything.

"You remind me of your father, you know." So seldom was the subject broached in his house that Jax found himself focusing, zooming in on what his mother was saying.

They were sitting on the couch in the living room, baby Jeffrey between them, softly cooing. Jax was making half-assed attempts to play with the kid, and the kid, as always, wasn't having it.

"How so, ma?"

"He was like that too. Held his emotions in close check. Love wasn't … wasn't easy for him."

"So, why'd you—" Jax stopped himself, but the unspoken question hung in the air between them. Why did you choose to love a man who didn't or couldn't love you back as much?

She smiled wistfully. "Oh, you know. I was young. Stupid. Thought I could change him. We think these things when we're young, don't we? Like people are projects or canvasses—unbound potential for us to uncover and shape to our liking. I guess I figured I had enough exuberant love for both of us."

Jax thought about it and told himself to tread carefully. "Were you happy?"

"For a while I was. I thought I was. And then you came along, and I was just over the moon. You were such a lovely baby, such a happy baby, you seldom even cried. All the other new moms I knew were stumbling around bleary-eyed from sleep deprivation, black bags under their eyes, always so tired, but you let me sleep through most nights pretty well. It's like we were a team, you and me."

She smiled at the reminiscence. We're still a team, Jax thought, though no longer by choice. Bet she didn't think she'd still be living with her baby all these years later. Still or again? Was there even a difference?

Instead, he asked, "Did Dad love me?"

"Of course, he did, hon. Of course, he loved you. He just had a hard time showing it. He just wasn't a naturally warm man, you know. He grew up an orphan, and I think all those foster homes really did a number on him. He wouldn't talk about it, but it was like he had PTSD or something. Like a lock on his heart."

"A lock on his heart," Jax echoed. It sounded like a great song title.

"I mean, not all love gets to be expressed all the time, does it?" His mom, the eternal optimist, always trying to see the best in everyone. "You love Jeffie, I know you do. Just like your dad loved you."

It took an effort to maintain a steady expression on his face. Shit, he hoped that wasn't the case, he hoped his father loved him more than that. Although, genetically speaking, he supposed it made sense. If such things were even bound by genetics. He got his dad's looks, why not his stony, reticent heart, too?

"He tried with you, just like you're trying with Jeffie. It just takes time, it takes patience."

"Sure didn't try long," Jax snapped before he could catch himself.

His mom frowned. "I know, hon, I know." She patted his hand affectionately. "I've made peace with him leaving a long time ago. And I hope you haven't been thinking it was ever your fault, any of it. Your dad was just one of those people, a rolling stone. There was a wind in his sails, though it never blew in any one direction for long."

Jax had no idea where his dad was. No one did. The man had taken off ages ago, leaving behind only some photos and some vague and distant memories. His disappearance wasn't legendary like that of Aaron Chase. It was much more ordinary and much less exciting—a cowardly slinking away into the night without so much as a good explanation. Jax didn't count a note on the back of a Shop-N-Go receipt left on the kitchen table that read "I'm sorry, I just can't anymore" as a good explanation. Jax didn't even find out about the note for years, and by then the wound of his father's abandonment had all but scabbed over. The resilience of youth and all that.

"You look so much like him, but I know you're not the same. I know your heart. You'll always do the right thing. You're good. You're my good boy."

His mom got like that sometimes, drunk on sentimentality. Jax didn't say a word, didn't tell her that he believed her to be wrong. He didn't think he was good; he didn't think he was evil—he believed everyone had it in them to be both given the right opportunity. He didn't ascribe any specific moral value to himself. Life was hard enough without additional labels and their concomitant expectations.

Jax's mom brushed away at her eyes with her thumbs and smiled. "Love you, kiddo," she said, and he wasn't sure if she meant him or the baby or both. Then she went to the kitchen to make some tea. Jax sighed and shook his head. "Grandpa was a jerk, wasn't he?" he addressed Jeffrey quietly. The baby burbled back. For a moment, they sat together quietly doing nothing at all. Then the baby started crying again.

One thing Donna was always good about was birthdays. Obsessively so. Every full-time employee got a card with a cheesy pun and a store-bought cake. While the cards were, presumably, secretly thrown into the trash; the cake got sliced into slivers of artificially flavored high-calorie cheer and distributed among the staff. Despite whatever current diet wave Donna was riding at the time, she always partook. It was like she read a management manual once and this was the main thing that stuck.

And so, of course, she remembered Jax's birthday this year. His card, addressed to Jackson, *of course*, featured a demented-looking squirrel and a pun he forgot immediately after reading it, and his cake was one of Stop-N-Go's finest confections in garish, unnatural-looking colors and a mountain of whipped cream for decoration.

A single unlit birthday candle stuck out of the middle. They couldn't light it because their hyper-sensitive smoke detectors would go ballistic. A lesson learned the hard way over the years.

The employees who were around that day gathered in the staffroom/cafeteria/vending machine zone and sang him an amusingly discordant Happy Birthday led by Donna, in volume if not tone. He mock-blew out the birthday candle, and Donna sliced out the cake to distribute it around on cheap paper plates.

Jax got to work so early that morning, he didn't see his mom in the kitchen. He was glad she got a chance to sleep in. He had all but forgotten the date, had she not left a plate of heart-shaped peanut butter raisin cookies out for him in a festive birthday tin.

He smiled; he had loved those cookies ever since he was

a kid and threw in a bunch of raisins into the baking mix while helping his mom in the kitchen. They certainly made for a delicious breakfast.

And now there was cake. He was going to be doing sugar-high jumping jacks at this rate. He ate as much as he could stomach, making sure Donna saw him enjoy it, and then disposed of the rest discreetly.

"Here," she handed him a plate with an extra slice. "You wanna take some to Mr. Chambers?"

"Sure. Thanks, Donna."

"You're doing a really good job with him." He waited for some lamentable follow-up, but none came.

"Um, thanks. Thank you." What is this, he thought, some kind of birthday niceness?

"He doesn't have much time left, you know."

"I figured." He didn't have to be an expert to guess. The old man was fading like a movie ghost right before his eyes, every single day. Jax didn't dare think of what would happen when he went.

"I hear you're playing to him. It's nice. Not my kind of music, but nice."

"What kind of music do you like?"

"Oh, you know, the Beatles."

"Everyone likes the Beatles." Jax said, smiling to ensure the words didn't come across condescendingly.

"Well, if you ever wanna play some music like that for our clients. I'm sure I could arrange that."

Ah. No. "Thanks, I'll keep it in mind."

"Well, I'll let you get back to work. I'm sure Mr. Chambers is expecting you."

Jax took the extra cake slice and left, feeling positively bewildered. That had to have been the first normal—and more importantly brief—conversation he'd ever had with Donna. He should have birthdays more often, he thought.

Mr. Chambers was indeed expecting him. He didn't say as much but he didn't have to. Over time Jax had learned to pick up on the old man's subtleties, minute expression changes and sighs and other tiny things a person too weighed down by his years to emote properly might resort to.

"Got you some cake," Jax smiled, presenting the slice with his best Vanna White impression.

The old man gestured that it was okay for Jax to feed him some. Jax did, maneuvering the plastic fork expertly. Plastic seemed undignified, but it was much safer to wield when feeding another person.

"Good?"

Mr. Chambers nodded ever so slightly and then again toward a water carafe. Jax poured him a glass, added a straw, and held it carefully at an appropriate angle.

The old man drank slowly, then pressed his thin lips together trapping a stray drop of water.

"Happy Birthday, Jax."

"Thanks. I almost forgot it was today." He wondered idly if Deek would remember or if their friendship had drifted too far now for minutiae.

"That's how you know you're getting old."

"Yeah, I guess so."

"How about a birthday story?"

"I'd love one if you're up for it."

"Let's give it a whirl and see." The old man seemed to be in good spirits. Whether he was buoyed by the occasion or by his impending release from this mortal coil was difficult to tell. But if he wanted to spend what time he had left telling stories, Jax would be happy to listen.

"Once upon a time, there was a young man who dreamed of rock'n'roll stardom."

Is this about me, Jax wondered?

"He had a guitar on his skin—" *Ah, not me, then.* "—and a guitar in his heart, and everywhere he went he heard music. Songs came easily to him, and they were good, but they were never great and what he wanted was greatness."

"Guess no one told him it was the enemy of good then, huh?" Jax joked. The old man gave him a brief I'm-amused-but-don't-interrupt smile and continued.

"Years were passing him, and greatness continued to elude him. And he became less and less satisfied with just being good. He sought to lose himself in different highs to counteract his existential lows, but nothing took. His desperation drove him to new extremes; he began dabbling in dark arts, doing esoteric research, playing around with black magic."

Whoa, thought Jax, this was getting trippy. The old man paused, he seemed exhausted, and he gestured to be given more water before he was ready to continue.

"In the end, all it took was an old legend—the devil at the crossroads. He went there at midnight and waited beneath the full moon. A demon came, and a pact was struck. Only that demon had high demands, and the man didn't have much to give him, so in the end, desperate and stupid, he gave him his youth. Traded away his years for a chance at perfection. They shook hands, and the demon's skin sliced straight through the man's hand, so that their pact was signed in blood. And so, it was done."

The old man paused. His expression unreadable. He seemed miles away. Slowly, he resumed his story.

"The next day the man woke up in his own bed and thought he had the strangest dream. But then he saw an already healed cut on his hand, touched the scar, and remembered. And then, he sat down and wrote the best song he had ever written. A perfect song. It hit the radio waves and took off like a wildfire in a drought. The day it charted on Billboard, the man found his first grey hair. It was all downhill from there, only so much more rapidly than he could have ever anticipated.

He didn't have much time to enjoy his fame. Guess he should have been more specific. Guess he should have asked more questions. But it was too late by then. And so, he took his newfound fortune, had his lawyers draw up contracts for royalties, and hid himself away from the world in plain sight. And there he stayed, awaiting his final day, lost in the memories of the life he'd once had and the music he'd once played."

The old man hung his head, exhausted. This was laborious for him—more words than Jax had ever heard him say at one time or maybe even altogether. Jax offered him more water, but he didn't even have the energy to drink, it seemed. Just sat there as if trying to slowly recharge.

The full weight of the story hit Jax gradually at first, and then all at once. This was a confirmation of all his suspicions, but much darker, much more Faustian than he had ever dreamed of. He had so many questions. But first…

"Are you okay, Mr. Chambers?" and then he dared,

"Aaron?"

The old man lifted his head. Jax could tell how much effort it took.

"I figured you'd want to know for sure, before … "

Jax nodded. "Thank you. I did. Thank you for telling me."

"Wait before you tell anyone, it won't be long now."

"I won't tell if you don't want me to."

The old man managed a slight shrug as if to say it didn't matter or maybe as if to say, "Who'd believe it anyway?"

Who would indeed? Jax thought. Maybe Tori.

"Do you know why I told you?"

"Cause you forgot to buy me a birthday cupcake?"

"Ha." The old man wheezed for a while then finally got his breath back. "I told you, so you don't do something stupid. I know you're unhappy…"

Jax shrugged as if it didn't matter.

The old man suddenly reached and grabbed his hand with surprising strength. Made eye contact.

"Jax, don't do anything stupid. Live your life as it comes to you. Take the discordant bits along with the melodic ones. Don't go looking for some mythical perfection."

Now that Jax knew the story behind it, he could feel the ridge of the scar on the old man's hand pressing into his skin. He smiled and, as gently as he could, retrieved his hand.

"I won't. I'll chug along, don't worry about me."

Mr. Chambers' watery eyes searched Jax's for a moment as if to make sure he was telling the truth and were apparently satisfied with what they found. Everyone always said Jax had a perfect poker face, though he hated poker.

"Well, then, I'm beat. Wanna play me your latest?"

"You bet," said Jax, reaching for the Martin. He played, and the old man drifted off to sleep, waking up only when it was time for Jax to leave for the day.

"That time?" he croaked weakly.

"I'll be back before you know it."

"Happy birthday, Jax."

"Thank you."

The old man nodded.

Jax lingered in the entryway and hesitated. "Can I just ask one question?"

Another nod.

"Was it ever…worth it? Was there ever a moment where it was just like…pure wow?"

The old man took so long in answering, Jax thought he had fallen back asleep, but no, he must have been just thinking.

He looked up at Jax and there was a smile on his face so radiant, so transformative, that for a second the years fell away and Jax could see his idol behind the time-ravaged features, Aaron Chase, the man, the legend. "There might have been one or two," he said quietly. Then he waved Jax away and turned to the window.

At that moment, Jax knew with absolute certainty that the old man wasn't admiring the cherry blossoms, then or ever;

that while he appeared to be looking out, he was, in fact, looking inwardly, into his past, retreating to that one perfect time he knew: those one or two pure wow instances, a high impossible to imitate, a high one could chase forever.

"Goodnight, Aaron Chase," Jax whispered and left.

The old man died that night. Passed away in his sleep, they said. Peacefully. Jax found out about it from Donna who, to her credit, did her best to stay respectful and subdued. She even took a beat before asking Jax if he wanted to stick with the attendant's work.

Shit, Donna, he thought. I'd buy you tact if I knew where they were selling it.

"You're good at it, and the money's better."

"I'll think about it, Donna," he promised.

Jax didn't need to think about it, though. He knew with dead certainty that he wasn't cut out for the gig, didn't have it in him to watch another person die. What he felt, he couldn't quite put into words, didn't have the emotional vocabulary for it. Something like sadness mixed with relief that came from knowing the old man was ready to go.

He hoped Aaron Chase's heaven was a never-ending rock'n'roll party, but given what he learned the night before, he wasn't sure heaven was the man's final destination.

Jax didn't know who he could possibly talk to about this. Deek would have been his first stop for years, but Deek of the drifting-apart birthday-forgetting friendship, he wasn't so certain about. He thought Tori might get it, but it didn't seem right to pry open those old scabbed-over wounds of hers. Funnily enough, the person he most wanted to talk to just then was the person he no longer would be able to talk to ever again.

He did the next best thing and cued up Aaron Chase's last anthem to play on repeat in his earbuds as he went back to his mop and bucket duties.

At the end of the day, Donna found him once again.

"Jackson, I almost forgot," she said, "Mr. Chambers left you something. I put it in your locker."

In his locker? Had this woman ever heard of boundaries?

"Okay, thanks, Donna."

It took considerable willpower not to book it to the lockers, but Jax steeled himself and walked at a measured pace. His fingers shook a little and it took three tries to get it unlocked. It was just big enough to accommodate the Martin -D28 Dreadnought guitar. There was a small note attached to it with some writing on it in a thin spiky cardiogram-looking script, as if the letters had taken a tremendous amount of effort to render. Jax knew they must have.

"Don't go chasing the enemy of good."

It was signed, too. Jax could make out C, H, A, and then a squiggly line. It could have been Chambers or Chase. It didn't really matter.

Jax picked up the guitar and closed his eyes. He didn't realize he was crying until another employee startled him by walking in and saying something. Jax couldn't remember the

last time he cried.

Life went back to normal too quickly. It seemed wrong. It was as if nothing had ever happened. Just a glitch in The Matrix and then normal programming resumed. For a brief while, Jax's life felt … he wasn't sure what, maybe more important somehow? Now he was back to being some guy that used to be in a band, before devolving into a lowly janitor and a useless dad.

If he was being honest with himself, he hated it. All of it. The endlessly dirty toilets, the chats with Donna, the cheap beer, the masochistic attendances of his former band's concerts, the endless optimistic cheer of his mom, the wails of the baby.

His mom swore the kid was starting to talk, but he was

yet to do it in front of Jax. He was crawling now, though, always crawling away from him.

Maggie's hours got cut at her latest job, and she was struggling to make the rent. Out of the boundless kindness of her heart, his mom offered her to stay with them until she got back on her feet. He couldn't even imagine how much shittier things would get if Maggie accepted, and she appeared to be leaning toward acceptance.

Jax could see in technicolor detail the entirety of his life unfolding in front of him with nothing to look forward to in it. Not a thing. He couldn't bear it.

The brightest moments of his days were spent with the Martin—the music was his only solace. He had enough original songs for an album now. An album no one would likely ever hear at this rate. Sure, his songs needed some touches here and there, but they were good, he knew. They finally shed the youthful angst and acquired the sort of verisimilitude that life beats into a person over time, a certain experiential authenticity.

Was he still a musician if there was no audience? It was a *tree falls in the woods* sort of a dilemma.

And then there was The Thought. That wild and crazy thought playing through his mind like a background track on repeat. The one he tried to shrug off during the day by keeping busy only to surrender to in the quiet hours of the night.

Jax had a friend with OCD once all the way back in middle school, and he remembered asking him what it was like. The way his friend described it then was similar to what Jax was experiencing now—a kind of a relentless tireless haunting. It wore you out to a shadow, and he knew it was only a matter of time.

There was no catalyst. Not really. It was just another tedious day in a procession of tedious days that comprised Jax's life when something in his mind just snapped. He could practically hear the snap, a jarringly discordant sound amid the steady drone of quotidian noises, and then he knew, he simply *knew* it was time.

He wore all black to blend in with the night. He didn't want to be seen; he even put his hood up. Jax, who had never gambled a day in his life, felt ready to spin the wheel. Or, more aptly, the cylinder of the revolver. He stood at the crossroads just outside of town, a full moon his only light.

Ready or not … Oh, but he was ready. He had thought about it, as much as he'd tried not to. He had scarcely thought of anything else. Jax might not have been the brightest candle in the chandelier, but he was smart enough to learn from his own mistakes and the mistakes of others. Didn't he get a vasectomy immediately after Maggie sprung the baby surprise on him? Didn't he think through all the details of his questions before even contemplating asking? The Devil, after all, was in the details.

Jax would never offer his youth; that was to be

proverbially wasted on him and him alone. He wasn't going to bargain away his soul either—he didn't think it'd be much of a bargain. He knew he didn't have much else to offer, but if all the horror movies he had watched over the years had taught him one thing only, it was the power of the firstborn. Demons seemed to find it irresistible. And he was simply too sad and tired to be good.

The night was starless; its beauty ominous. Jax tried to think of a chord progression for it as he waited. The wind picked up and it rustled through the trees, providing its own discordant notes to the melody. Jax closed his eyes. Something was coming.

ACKNOWLEDGEMENTS

This book child took a very small village but dedicated village to raise, and I'm very grateful to everyone who helped make the story I dreamt up into a printed reality. So, here's gratitude where gratitude is due:

To Tony Anuci of Anuci Press for bringing the book back in print and giving it such a lovely home.

To Arthur Shattuck O'Keefe, a wonderful author and a better friend, for editing assistance, a wonderful blurb.

To J.G. Faherty, whose books I've been reading for ages, for taking the time to read and very generously praise *Discordant*. It even made his top 3 books of 2023.

To Jim Ody, talented and tattooed and terrific, for all the lovely, amazing, phenomenally flattering things he said about my writing in general and *Discordant* specifically.

To Atticus Morton, my awesome superfan, for continuously buoying my spirits and creating the first ever (as far as I know) dedicated Mia Dalia bookshelf.

D I S C O R D A N T

To Davida De La Harpe Golden for all her invaluable help and eagle eye.

To everyone who buys, reads, and promotes my work. Thank you, thank you, thank you!

And last but not least, my boundless gratitude to my beautiful wife, Chelsea, who saves my world from being discordant.

ABOUT THE AUTHOR

Mia Dalia is an internationally published author, a lifelong reader, and a longtime reviewer of all things fantastic, thrilling, scary, and strange.

Short fiction credits: Night Terror Novels, 50-word stories, Flash Fiction Magazine, Pyre Magazine, Tales from the Moonlit Path and in print anthologies by Sunbury Press, HellBound Press, Black Ink Fiction, Dragon Roost Press, Unsettling Reads, Moon, Anthology of Lunar Horror, Phobica Books, Psycho Toxin Press, Wandering

Wave Press, Bullet Points vol. 3, Critical Blast, Sinister Smile Press, DraculaBeyondStoker Magazine, Mystery Magazine, Headshot Press, Zoetic Press' Alphanumeric, and Tales to Terrify (awarded runner-up in best of 2023).

Upcoming: Short fiction will appear in anthologies by Nightshade Press, Off-Topic Publishing, Exploding Head Press, Book Slayer Press, RebellionLIT, Grendel Press, and Crystal Lake Publishing.

Novellas: *Tell Me a Story* and *Discordant* (Psychotoxin Press originally). Anuci Press currently.

Upcoming: *Arrokoth* (Spaceboy Books)

Novels: *Estate Sale* (Black Ink Fiction)

Upcoming: *Haven* (CamCat Books)

Collections: *Smile So Red and Other Tales of Madness* (Anuci Press)

Find her at

Official website: https://daliaverse.wixsite.com/author

Twitter: @ Dalia_Verse

FB: DaliaVerse

Instagram: daliaverse

https://linktr.ee/daliaverse

If you enjoyed this book, kindly consider leaving a rating and a review on Amazon, Goodreads, or a website of your choosing. Shout it from the rooftops, skywrite it, get creative.

Trust me, there's no easier and better way to make an author happy and show your appreciation as a reader!

Although this particular author also responds to baked goods!